Strange

Strange Tales Book One

Iris Carden

Published by: Iris Carden
   Ipswich, Qld, Australia
   iriscardenauthor.blog

ISBN: 978-0-6459679-6-8

A catalogue record for this work is available from the National Library of Australia.

Cover Art: Wine and Wand by Iris Carden

Contents

Hello, Dear Reader

Hello, dear Reader, I am the Narrator, here to tell you stories of strangeness.

Sometimes, they'll involve magic. Sometimes, someone will learn something. Sometimes, a person will get what they richly deserve.

One thing I can guarantee, all of these stories will be strange.

Are you ready? Then on to our first story of strangeness…

Hey Siri

Hello dear Reader. I invite you to get comfortable now, while I tell you the strange tale of Gertrude who lived the high life, for a little while.

Gertrude was your average overweight, middle aged, divorced single woman. Life had played her a tough hand, but she'd managed to survive all that had been thrown at her, so far.

Gertrude loved technology, at least she loved the technology that could make her life easier. She loved her smart watch and the smart phone it was linked to. She loved that so much of her house could be linked to these devices. To turn on lights or the television, or even open the front gate, she just had to say: "Hey Siri," and give the command.

While much of her life was in disarray, at least those things which could be controlled from her watch or phone were well under control.

Then came the day of the big storm. Gertrude had seen her wheelie bin blown down the street in the wild winds, so she rushed outside to chase it. Don't go out in a storm, dear Reader, bad things can happen, just as they did to Gertrude. She was struck by lightning.

She awoke at the local hospital, where ambulance officers watched over patients while waiting to hand them over to the overworked Emergency Department staff.

Gertrude didn't know why she did it, but she lifted her wrist, and said to her watch, "Hey Siri, get me some treatment so I can go home."

The voice of the watch replied: "Working on it."

Less than a minute later a nurse came to collect her. A brief check, some treatment for minor burns, and she was released, to go back home.

That night, Gertrude lay awake, wondering: did the watch bring her the immediate treatment, or would it have happened anyway? Another thing bothered her. After a whole day without being recharged, the watch was still on a hundred percent charge.

She finally decided she would test whether the watch had gained some new strange power. "Hey Siri," she said, "make me a healthy weight by morning."

The voice of her watch answered: "You got it."

Gertrude finally slept, and then she woke. She found that overnight she had lost at least forty kilograms. Loose skin hung like an elephant's all over her.

"Hey Siri," she said, "tighten my skin so it suits my new body."

The electronic voice answered: "Working on it."

She felt a tingle, and went to stand in front of a full-length mirror, watching, amazed, as her skin pulled itself taut.

What power she had at her disposal! She thought a moment that her watch had become like God. Then she realised it was not the same at all. God could, and often did, simply say "No" without any kind of explanation. A smart watch could only do as it was commanded, or say: "I'm unable to do that at the moment."

Perhaps it was more like Aladdin's genie, and was a powerful supernatural slave. Something nagged at the back of her mind, something she had heard about jinn not being all that benevolent. She pushed the nagging thought aside.

That night was a big lotto draw. It had jackpotted to two hundred million dollars. Gertrude decided her new shape could definitely do with a new wardrobe, and new living conditions.

"Hey Siri, make my lotto entry win."

"Working on it."

Of course she won.

The next day she bought a mansion and a new car. While waiting for the thirty days for the purchase of the house to be finalised, Gertrude bought herself the most beautiful and expensive clothes she could find.

For five years, Gertrude lived the high life. Big donations to charity, and to cultural and sporting groups gained her invitations to gala events. She knew and was known by all the "best" people, "best" in this case meaning wealthiest, and she lived large. If she was, in her quieter times, lonely, and concerned about what the downside of her using supernatural powers might be, that was hidden from the world.

She no longer asked anything outrageous of her watch, simply the normal everyday things of turning lights on and off, keeping her appointments diary, all the things a smart watch normally did. It still stayed at full charge without ever being recharged, a constant reminder to her that it was not a normal smart watch.

Then came the day, when her watch notified her of only one appointment for the day: "Die".

She looked at it, looked again. It had to be a glitch. "Hey Siri," she said, "what are my appointments for the day?"

The electronic voice answered her: "Nine am, die. All other appointments have been cancelled."

It was 8.30am. She had half an hour, and didn't know what to do with it. She was in good health, she knew. What was supposed to happen in half an hour?

She decided to stay home for the day, not to go out, not to take any unnecessary risks.

With nothing else to do, she went for a swim in her backyard pool.

You've heard lightning never strikes the same place twice. That's not actually true, dear Reader. Lightning often strikes the same place more than once. Sometimes it even strikes the same person twice.

Gertrude was enjoying her heated salt-water pool, when stormclouds appeared out of nowhere. The lightning strike not only hit her directly, but also travelled through the pool water. She was electrocuted from two sources simultaneously. This time there was no ambulance ride. This time her heart stopped instantly.

And so, dear Readers, ends the story of Gertrude, but I wonder what happened to the morgue assistant who stole a smart watch from the body.

Hypnotherapy

Hello again dear Reader. I invite you to get comfortable now, while I tell you the strange tale of Elizabeth, who went to get help with a bad habit, and developed another instead.

Elizabeth had a terrible problem with falling for the wrong men, the kind of men who would take advantage of her and mistreat her. She decided the problem was her lack of self-esteem, her willingness to accept less than acceptable behaviour from the men she allowed in her life.

Friends recommended a hypnotherapist who had a reputation for being sympathetic, and providing a great deal of help to clients.

The hypnotherapist welcomed her, and offered her a comfortable arm chair. He got her a coffee while they talked about what she wanted from the session.

Then he pulled a stool over closer, and sat directly in front of her. He began speaking in a slow, gentle, melodious tone, and Elizabeth felt herself drifting into another state of consciousness.

Now, dear Reader, they say you can't be hypnotised to do something you don't want to do. But what was in that drink the hypnotherapist had given Elizabeth? It certainly wasn't only coffee. Could whatever it was have made her even more suggestible?

As if from a vast distance, Elizabeth heard the hypnotherapist's voice instruct her to go to a certain place, and shoot a man he described.

Elizabeth felt a handgun pressed into her hand. She wanted to say "no", to resist his instruction, but her body seemed to act of its own accord. Even in her disassociated state, Elizabeth felt her heart beat faster, her stomach tighten, her bowels turn to water and demand the release they were not granted. She poured sweat, but still her body obeyed the instructions.

She walked into a crowded coffee shop, and saw the man the hypnotist had described. She wanted to yell a warning, but her throat was closed up and would let no words escape. She wanted to turn and run, but her feet would not obey her command. She was desperate not to do this, but she did it. She fired the gun, saw the man go down, and she turned and deliberately walked back to the hypnotherapist's consulting room.

She sat back on the comfortable chair. The therapist removed the gun from her hand and placed on a cabinet in the corner of the room.

The slow, melodious voice said, "I am going to count down from ten when I reach one, you will be fully awake and you will remember nothing of what has happened."

"Ten."

Elizabeth still felt her heart beating, seemingly a thousand times its normal speed.

"Nine."

She still wanted to run, but her body was still frozen in place.

"Eight."

How could this supposed professional abuse his trust in this manner?

"Seven."

Fear was turning into rage. Her heart pumped yet faster. But the weak, watery feeling in her gut was turning to cold, hard, steel.

"Six."

Once more she'd trusted a man who mistreated her and used her for his own ends.

"Five."

Her mind closed on a simple idea: "It stops now."

"Four."

No-one would ever take advantage of her again.

"Three."

She would see to it that everyone who had abused her trust would pay.

"Two."

And it would start with this man in front of her.

"One. Wake up. You do not remember anything."

She remembered everything, but now she had control over her body. Before the hypnotherapist could register what was happening, she'd run across the room, grabbed the gun, turned and shot him.

She opened the drawers of the cabinet and searched until she found extra bullets for the gun.

There were a lot of men who had taken advantage of her, and they were all going to answer for it.

So, dear Reader, we leave Elizabeth, who really was cured of her tendency to fall for the wrong kind of men. No-one will ever take advantage of her again.

Witch

Settle in dear Reader, while I tell you the strange tale of Ellie, who put on a costume and become someone else entirely.

Ellie had seen the new shop on her way to school. It was called "Magique Mystique" and had witches' costumes, brooms, cauldrons, and all other kind of witch paraphernalia.

Being a diligent student, and a wider reader, Ellie knew witches hadn't really been magical at all. They had just been women who were punished for not fitting in with the patriarchal culture of their day. She didn't know how many customers Magique Mystique would draw, but it was nice to think of someone celebrating women who had been ostracised.

Women, in whatever era, who claimed their power, were enviable in Ellie's mind. She never felt any power of her own. Ellie wished she could defy the powers that ruled her life.

Like the long-past witches, she was also ostracised in her culture. Her culture being the school community. All her life she'd been a target for bullies, and ignored by the other girls. Perhaps that was why she was so well-read for her seventeen years of age. Books had never mistreated her yet.

When Kirsty invited her to the halloween costume party, Ellie was surprised. She'd never been invited to one of Kirsty's parties before, and Kirsty was dating Ben, the biggest bully of them all.

Ellie surprised herself by accepting the invitation. She knew there was probably something horrible planned for her, some new and awful way to humiliate her, but she couldn't give up the tiny seed of hope that perhaps Kirsty actually wanted to be her friend.

There's a lesson here dear Reader: never trust a serpent to be anything other than a serpent.

Ellie knew exactly the costume she wanted. She went to Magique Mystique, and there she found a long black dress with red trim and a red tied belt. A witches' hat with the same red trim. An old-fashioned straw broom, a wooden wand which wasn't quite straight, and even clunky, silver-buckled old fashioned shoes.

The cashier told her the red trim was for senior witches, novices wore all black. Ellie laughed and said she be a senior witch for the night.

As the cashier carefully wrapped the wand in tissue paper, she said, "Be careful where you point this and be clear in your intent."

Ellie laughed it off. It was a prop, a toy, and had no real power, after all.

When Ellie arrived at the backyard party, she found her classmates dressed as ghosts and ghouls, monsters and witches, but none had a costume anywhere near as authentic as hers. She was glad she hadn't just gone to some lame costume shop and bought whatever they had.

Her authentic-looking costume made her feel somehow more confident, more sure of herself, more powerful.

Ben approached her. Inwardly she groaned, then steeled herself for whatever was coming.

"I always knew you were a witch," he said. He emphasised "witch" in a way that made it obvious he meant a similar, rhyming, word.

"And I always knew you," and here she pointed the wand to emphasise the "you", "were a toad."

Then it happened. There was a sudden blaze of light, so bright it was all anyone could see. It was over in a moment, and Ben's clothes lay, seemingly empty on the floor. As everyone's eyes adjusted to the normal light again, the clothing moved slightly, and a fat cane toad crawled out.

"Ellie, what happened?" Kirsty asked.

Ellie turned her head slowly toward Kirsty. "What year is this?" she asked

"It's twenty twenty-four," Kirsty said in a voice that suggested it had been a stupid question.

"Twenty twenty-four," Ellie repeated. "I've been gone three hundred and seventy-six years."

"Ellie, what are you talking about?"

"I don't know this Ellie you speak of. My name is Agatha. I was executed in sixteen forty-eight."

"You were, what?"

"I was hanged by Matthew Hopkins, the Witch Finder General."

"Ellie, you're crazy."

"Crazy? Perhaps Ellie is, but I am not."

She sat on the broom, kicked off against the ground and flew into the night. After centuries, she had much to learn about the world. Perhaps she'd let this Ellie back from time to time to help her learn what had changed. Perhaps she would not.

Aggie Waters was a senior witch, and she had her wand back now. She did not need help from the weak girl whose body she inhabited.

And so dear Reader, we leave Ellie, wherever she has gone. Her costume is indeed incredibly authentic, and has given her so much power. It's a pity she'll never know about it. As for the shop Magique Mystique, no-one ever saw it in that place again. But it will appear dear Reader, because Aggie Waters misses her coven.

Kevin

Settle in dear Reader while I tell you the strange tale of Margaret, who wanted a pet for companionship, but found herself with something unexpected.

After the break-up of her marriage, Margaret was lonely. She'd been kept isolated from her friends and family for a long time, and only realised it now she was alone and had to try to rebuild some of the damaged relationships.

Feeling overwhelmed and alone, Margaret decided to get a pet, a companion animal who would keep her company. She opted to go to a shelter, to find a pet who needed her as much as she needed it.

She'd gone expecting to find a cat or a small dog. She left with a sulfur crested cockatoo named Kevin. Staff at the shelter told her Kevin could talk, in fact he'd been returned to the shelter several times because potential owners had not liked the things he said.

Margaret knew birds didn't understand the things they said, they just mimicked what they'd heard humans say. If he said inappropriate things, her lack of social life gave her plenty of time to teach him to say something new.

Kevin was soon set up in a corner of the lounge room, with a cage that was kept open when Margaret was home and could make sure he didn't get into any danger. He had a big perch, and plenty of toys.

"Who's a pretty birdie?" Margaret said.

"You've got to be kidding me," Kevin replied.

"Kevin want a cracker?"

"Nah. Have you got a bit of apple or sunflower seeds?" Then he began to recite The Man from Snowy River.

If Margaret hadn't known better, she would have believed Kevin knew what he was saying.

Humans are arrogant, dear Reader, we often think ourselves smarter than other forms of life. Margaret was about to learn she'd misjudged this bird.

On Monday morning, Margaret said to the cockatoo. "OK Kevin, I'm off to work. You're going to have to go into your cage for a while."

Kevin replied, "Drive carefully. You never know when a tyre's going to blow out."

It was a very strange thing for anyone to teach a bird to say, but the shelter had prepared her to hear odd things from Kevin.

Margaret's house was on the outskirts of town, and it took her twenty minutes to drive to work. As she was driving on a fairly quiet stretch of road, a semi-trailer came up close behind her. Margaret watched the huge truck in her rear view mirror, and mentally willed the driver to back off. The truckie, of course, did nothing of the sort.

Then her front passenger-side tyre blew. As she fought to wrest control of the steering, the truckie tried to slow down, and failed, hitting the back of her car and sending her spinning off the side of the road. Her car came to rest against a fence, as the truck hurtled past, only to slow and stop further up the road.

Margaret was unhurt, but dazed, when the truck driver called an ambulance. After a brief visit to the hospital emergency department, she was cleared to go home.

The next day, as Margaret put Kevin in the cage, before she went outside to await a taxi to work, Kevin said: "Severe weather warning. Torrential rains. High winds. Hail."

Margaret thought Kevin must have listened to a weather report at some time.

In the office that day, Margaret had a lot of work to catch up on, after missing the previous day. As she closed one client's file and returned it to the file room, she glanced out the window, and noticed the dark, heavy clouds gathering, and the sky taking on that miserable greenish tint of impending hail. Trees in the park across the road were bending low with the strength of the wind.

She chose another file from the secure file room and took it back to her desk. Outside, a lightning strike hit transformer on the overhead power pole adjacent the building, as a massive boom of thunder sounded, sparks flew, and the power went out. Margaret and her co-workers were left sitting in darkness, with no access to their computers.

The manager told the staff to lock whatever files they were working on in the file room and go home for the day.

Gail, a co-worker offered to drive Margaret home, an offer she gladly accepted. As they were travelling along the same road where Margaret had suffered her accident the previous day, the rain began. It didn't start gently, but with a sudden dump of water. It was as if they were driving through a waterfall. The wipers swished at their highest speed, but visibility was minimal. Then the hail began. Great rocks of ice thumped the car, and one smashed the windscreen. They were less than a block from Margaret's house when the windscreen smashed, so Gail continued to drive slowly, carefully, with her head out the driver's side window to see. As they arrived, sodden, at Margaret's house, Margaret suggested Gail park in the carport, and they wait the storm out inside.

They sat in the darkened house, with no power there either. Kevin dozed in his cage while they talked about the strange weather which had come out of nowhere. Gail said the morning weather report had been for sunny skies.

"I had a weather report that predicted this," Margaret said. "Kevin mimicked a severe weather warning. That bird says the weirdest things."

"You could earn real money with a psychic parrot," Gail said. Both women laughed.

Margaret opened Kevin's cage on her way to the kitchen. She put a saucepan of water on the gas stove, and made tea for them both, while Gail made the necessary phone calls.

Kevin woke up, saw his wire door was open, and climbed out to sit on top of the cage.

Gail called her car insurance company, and then her husband. The weather was affecting the mobile signal, and neither conversation was especially clear. She got the message across as best she could.

Kevin ruffled his feathers, and said in a sinister tone: "The visitor won't make it home."

"What?" Margaret said.

Kevin sang a verse of Waltzing Matilda.

The storm settled. Gail made her calls a second time. A tow truck came for her car, and her husband came for her.

At work the next day, she heard the news. Gail and her husband had stopped at a fast-food place to eat on the way home. A man with a gun and a mask had come in to rob the place, and Gail had been shot and died instantly.

Margaret thought back to what Kevin had said. Once or twice predicting things that actually happened could be coincidence, but surely not three times. She was beginning to understand why Kevin had been returned to the shelter so many times.

Her ex-husband called her at work. He wasn't supposed to do that, and she was angry. Ben insisted that he be allowed to come to the house that night to collect some things he believed should be his. He'd already taken most of the things they'd owned together, and she had simply allowed him to do so, and bought replacements, accepting it as the cost of him getting out of her life.

He hadn't been able to get the house, because it belonged to her grandmother, whose nursing home Margaret paid rent for. Margaret was grateful for that, as Ben had cost her so much.

Margaret decided he'd taken enough. She said no.

When she got home, he was there. Of course he was there. Her saying no hadn't meant anything while they were together, there was no reason it would do so now.

She had changed the locks, but he pushed past her as she went inside.

"Hello loser," Kevin said, as Ben entered the lounge room.

"Hey, a talking bird," Ben said. "That's so cool. Tell you what. Instead of the stuff I came for how about I take the bird? Let me have the bird and I promise I'll never bother you again."

Margaret thought about Kevin's three predictions of terrible things, and how scared she was of whatever he would say next. Then she thought Kevin didn't deserve to be left with someone as inconsiderate as Ben.

"I'm going with the loser," Kevin said.

"Really?" Margaret asked, realising she was now conversing with a cockatoo as if the bird actually understood what it was saying.

"I'm going to have fun with the loser," Kevin said, then began to recite, "I had written him a letter, which I had for want of better knowledge, sent to where I met him....."

Margaret left Kevin to his rendition of Clancy of the Overflow, and turned to Ben. "I guess Kevin's decided. He wants to go with you."

"His name's Kevin?"

"Yes. You have to clean his cage and change his water every day. He likes sunflower seeds, chopped apple, and reciting Banjo Patterson."

"You know, he doesn't know what he's saying don't you?"

"I thought I knew that, before I met him," Margaret said, "but I've come to wonder about that. If he wants to go with you, I'll pack up his stuff. But remember, you promised, you get nothing else. In fact, I want you to write that down and sign it."

She handed him a notebook and pen. He wrote the note, as directed, and signed it.

Margaret helped carry Kevin's food, toys and cage to Ben's car.

"Good-bye Kevin. It's been an adventure. I hope you like your new home."

"Get a cat," Kevin answered. "You'll like a cat."

So dear Reader, Margaret's adventures with Kevin are over. She's taken his advice and got a lovely ginger cat, named Marmalade. Marmalade's another shelter animal. She's old and only got one eye, but she's a sweet cat who loves to cuddle.

Ben's adventures are about to begin.

Cult

Settle in dear Reader while I tell you the strange tale of Julie, who inherited a nice house in a neighbourhood that wasn't as nice as it seemed.

Julie had mixed feelings the day she moved into her grandmother's old home. Of course she was delighted to finally have a home of her own, and not have to answer to landlords anymore. She was also sad, and quite horrified that her lovely grandmother had been murdered in that very same home.

Police had called her grandmother's killing a "robbery gone wrong," and had failed to apprehend the offender. Julie could not imagine a robbery going right, and regularly called the police to ask for updates on their investigation. Eventually the detective in charge had threatened to charge her with harassment if she kept calling.

In recent years, Julie had been visiting most weekends to help her grandmother manage the house and garden, so she knew most of the neighbours by sight, if not to speak to.

The house was an old Queenslander, with wide verandahs all around, and the shade helped to keep the interior of the house cool. Julie found the verandah a comfortable place to sit and read, or look at old photos and remember her grandmother.

Julie took a break from unpacking, and was sitting on the front verandah, lost in a book, when the woman who lived next door dropped by to visit. The woman invited Julie to her church. Julie politely declined, explaining quite honestly that she was still close enough to go to her old church, the one her grandmother had gone to as well. The neighbour told her everyone in the street went to the Church of the Enlightened Mind, and if Julie wanted to fit in, she would need to go there too, and invited her to think about it. She insisted on giving

Julie a note with her phone number on it so Julie could call her when she wanted to go.

Julie considered the whole encounter odd, but then recalled her grandmother telling her the neighbourhood had changed as her generation were dying, and some very strange people were moving in, and many were pressuring her to join a cult.

Well, dear Reader, this was not the last odd encounter she would have.

The next day a pushy woman in a business suit rang her doorbell. The woman's name was Gerda Swanston, and she was a real estate agent. She told Julie she had a buyer waiting who would pay above market price for her house. Julie explained she'd just moved in and wasn't planning to sell. Gerda Swanston then asked if Julie planned to join the Church of the Enlightened Mind. Julie said she was not. The real estate agent explained that everyone in the street was a part of the church, and she really ought to join, or sell to someone who would. Julie closed the door in her face.

Looking out the window, to ensure the woman was gone, Julie saw her across-the-street neighbour getting into his car to go to work for the day. She realised it was the detective investigating her grandmother's murder. Or was he the detective who was not investigating her grandmother's murder? Was he also a part of this church?

Julie worked from home, and had turned one of the bedrooms into an office. From there, she could see out over the back yard, at the many fruit trees and, ornamental trees, her grandparents had planted years before. A couple of rainbow lorikeets were there drinking nectar from a drunken parrot tree, and having a great time doing it.

She thought she heard a sound at the front of the house, and went out to find on the verandah floor, a hand-stitched calico doll, with button eyes, and three pins in its chest.

She picked the doll up and turned it over, noting that it was so badly made it could have represented a seal as easily as a human, and there was nothing personal about it at all, nothing to represent anyone.

Walking back to her office via the verandah, she was in for a horrible shock. The rainbow lorikeets were on the back verandah, dead, blood smeared over the floor and the back door of her house. Killing innocent, if mildly intoxicated, birds seemed to Julie an extreme offence. It had been done so quickly and quietly. She'd only been at the front of the house for a couple of minutes.

Julie was done with the nonsense. She pulled the pins out of the doll, thinking what amateurs these people really were. Didn't they know the doll wouldn't work without something to relate it to the person they were hexing? She found the business card the detective had given her when he'd spoken to her about her grandmother's death, the real estate agent's business card, and the note the next door neighbour had written with her phone number. She stuck a pin through each of them, and into the doll's chest.

Three heart attacks should be enough to persuade the Church of the Enlightened Mind to leave her alone. If not, she was capable of doing them far more harm.

Oh, dear Reader, did Julie say she was still going to her grandmother's church? That was the wrong word. The right word was "coven." She meant to say she was still going to her grandmother's coven.

Reality

Settle in dear Reader while I tell you the strange tale of Hilda, who had an accident, and then had a reality check.

Hilda was having a bad day. Her car wouldn't start. She'd had to call the breakdown service for a jump start, but they told her the battery needed to be replaced. After shuffling money from her savings account to her working account, she was able to pay for the battery and leave for work late.

She was doing her best to ignore the ringing mobile phone. It had to be her boss ringing to yell at her, although she'd already called to explain why she'd be late.

Don't drive while you're stressed and distracted, dear Reader, it could end very badly. It was a lesson Hilda learned when she failed to notice a red light and a pedestrian.

At least Hilda didn't just drive off. She stopped and ran to help the woman she's struck.

"You idiot!" The woman said as Hilda helped her to her feet. "You've broken my wing."

"Wing? Do you mean arm? Do you think your arm is broken? Do you need an ambulance?"

"No, fool. I'm fae. You've broken my wing."

"Fae? As in fairy? But fairies don't exist."

"Don't exist! Right my foolish young woman, you're about to find out what does and doesn't exist."

Hilda's eyes felt as if they were burning, and the world went blurry for a moment. When she could see again, the woman, the fae, did indeed have wings. They were incredibly fine, and patterned as if they were made of spiderweb.

A bigger shock would arrive with the police officers who came to investigate the accident. One was a tall young man and the other was short, with a lumpy face, pointed lumpy ears and a long, pointed, lumpy nose. Hilda screamed at the sight. The fairy whispered, "Goblin."

The Goblin police officer got the details of the accident, and issued Hilda with a notice to appear in court the next day for a dangerous driving charge. Her keys were taken from her and her car towed to a police holding yard.

Tearful, almost hysterical, Hilda rang her boss to ask for the day off. The boss growled at her that she was to come in to work, and leave her personal problems at home.

She caught a taxi, and arrived at work four hours late. Her boss, always a nasty and hairy guy, now had extra long hair, sharp pointed teeth, and large frightening claws. Hilda lost control. She screamed and screamed and screamed, fell on the floor and was totally incapable of anything but continuing to scream.

She was taken by ambulance to hospital, and left, still sobbing, in a room with several other people while waiting to see a doctor.

A television was on the wall, where someone was interviewing a well-known billionaire. The billionaire, however, wasn't human. He was a dragon, with thick shiny scales and long teeth, and long claw-like fingers. Why did everyone suddenly have sharp teeth and claws? The dragon was angry and spat fire with every word, while it sat in its pile of gold.

Hilda went from sobbing back to screaming, to shaking, repeating, "no, no, no, no, no" over again.

The doctor who finally saw her, had flawless, but sparkly, skin, and pointed ears. Hilda shrank back in her chair, covered her face and cried, occasionally saying incomprehensible things.

The kind doctor ordered something to calm her down, while admitting her to a ward until her condition could be stabilised.

There's not much chance of her recovering from her delusion any time soon, dear Reader. The charge nurse on her ward's a real ogre.

Elf

Settle in dear Reader, while I tell you the strange tale of Beatrice, who dreamed of being someone she wasn't, only to find the grass isn't always greener on the other side of the fence.

Beatrice was a low-level office worker, who had only one interest outside her boring office job. She loved fantasy fiction. She loved fantasy books. She loved fantasy movies. She even loved fantasy television series.

She often imagined herself as a powerful elf, along the lines of Galadriel, a great elf leader in Tolkein's stories, bearer of a magical ring of power.

The elf she dreamed of being was almost exactly the opposite of her real self. Beatrice did not make friends easily, or at all. She was uncomfortably shy, very insecure, and always felt like a fraud.

When it was announced that the work Christmas party that year would be fancy dress, she knew exactly what costume she would wear. With a long blond wig, a shiny satin dress, fake pointy ears, coloured contact lenses, and a fine golden-coloured crown, she transformed herself into an elf.

While dressed like an elf queen, she felt she could also put on the personality of the character. Let's face it dear Reader, that was a great improvement because she didn't have much of a personality of her own.

A co-worker approached her and said, "Hey, I don't think I've met you before."

She replied, "It's me, Bea, I've had the desk beside yours for two years, Evan."

"Really? I don't know how I didn't notice."

Beatrice went to find herself a drink. Along the way, she met someone she couldn't identify, dressed in a Santa suit.

"Great costume," the stranger said. "You like elves, do you?"

Something about him invited confidence. She told him about how her life was boring, and how she often dreamed of the being an elf, of the life she would lead.

"And if your dream could come true, would you really want it to?" Santa asked.

It only took her a moment's thought to answer in the affirmative.

Santa offered her a drink. Beatrice knew better than to accept drinks from men she didn't know, but something about Santa made her feel safe, and she accepted.

That was a big mistake. She almost immediately felt weak, the room seemed to be moving around her, colours blurred, and she passed out.

She woke up to find someone shaking her. She had been lying in a bed of straw in what appeared to be a factory of some sort.

"Get up lazybones," someone with a squeaky voice said. It was a small person in red trousers, a green shirt, and a red Santa cap.

As this person slowly came into focus, Bea asked the obvious question, "Where am I?" Her voice was also high pitched and squeaky. She looked down and realised she was dressed the same as the person who'd woken her. As she carefully stood up, she seemed closer to the floor than usual.

"We're in Santa's workshop, of course," the elf who had spoken to her said. "It's almost Christmas we've got to get these toys out, get to work."

And so Beatrice found herself on a production line among Santa's elves, making and wrapping toys for Christmas.

Nobody talked to her much on the production line, there was no time. They were working sixteen hour days.

One day, Beatrice tried to leave, and managed to get out of the building, only to find a desolate, snow-covered landscape, and a reindeer with a glowing nose munching on some hay from a feeder.

So dear Reader, Beatrice has achieved her fantasy and become an elf. Perhaps next Christmas, she'll ask Santa for her boring old life back.

Boxing Day

Settle in dear Reader while I tell you the story of Betty who was under-appreciated and wished for a different life.

Christmas Day had been the usual chaos. Betty had cooked for her own two children, her husband, her brother, sister-in-law, nieces and nephews, her father, and a couple of his elderly friends who'd had nowhere else to go for the day.

Everyone had eaten her work in no time, and no-one had bothered to thank her. Then they'd all ripped open the presents she'd spent weeks thoughtfully shopping for and wrapping. The thanks were minimal and mumbled. Her gift, bought by her husband, had been his own favourite chocolates.

Betty had been exhausted at the end of the day, and, after filling the dishwasher with the final load, had decided to leave the wrapping paper piled up to deal with on Boxing Day.

Now it was Boxing Day. No-one had magically decided to clean up the mess in the meantime. Picking up the discarded wrapping and cards, Betty found an envelope addressed to her which she hadn't seen before.

She opened and inside she found a card which said: "Good for one wish. Write your wish here."

It was a strange thing, but Betty appreciated that someone had thought of her. She found a pen and wrote in the blank space: "I wish I lived in old-fashioned times, in a fancy house where there were servants."

The room around her seemed to melt. She found herself kneeling on a hard, cold, stone floor. Her knees hurt and her back ached. There was a rash on her hands.

The light around her was multi-coloured, and when she looked up, she saw a beautiful stained-glass window set in the brick wall. Looking down, she saw she was wearing a

31

long, but very plain dress, and an apron. Beside her on the floor was a bucket of soapy water and a scrubbing brush.

"Off with the fairies again, are you girl?" A harsh voice behind her said.

She looked around and saw a woman dressed similarly to herself.

"Get back to work or you'll be on the streets," the woman said.

Well, dear Reader, you can imagine Betty's shock and regret. She thought about that wish, and the simple fact she hadn't added that she wanted to be the lady of the manor.

She thought about that tiny omission constantly as she scrubbed, and washed and cleaned and ironed for the rest of her life.

Betty's story is sad, of course, but spare a thought, dear Reader, for a servant girl, who suddenly found herself with no explanation in Betty's life, with modern appliances to help her, and with Betty's unappreciative husband and kids who didn't even notice the change.

Rock

Settle in, dear Reader, while I tell you the strange tale of Paula, who thought her opinion mattered more than anyone else's.

Paula was famous, mostly for expressing herself very loudly and offensively. Her long-suffering assistant Carol did her best to regulate the verbal diarrhoea that found its way to the media.

Paula's latest obsession was the Rock. It had had a perfectly respectable English name ever since it had been discovered. Now Aboriginal people wanted to change the name to some made-up word. Worse, they wanted to prevent people from climbing on it, ignoring the tourist industry and the freedom of people like her to do anything they felt like.

"To be fair, they discovered it, and named it, long before any white person did," Carol said.

"That's utter nonsense, and you know it. They say it's some special religious site. It's not like it's a cathedral or any building at all really. It's just a rock. It's a bloody great big rock in the middle of the desert. It's nothing."

"If it's nothing, why are you so upset about it?" Carol asked.

"You're supposed to be my assistant, not attacking me!" Paula yelled.

"Just asking what the media will ask when you inevitably say that publicly. So why are you upset about this rock you say is nothing?"

"Right, well. If we're practicing for the media, then it's because it's just another part of this woke culture, taking away our rights. White people are going to be second class citizens in our own country. You know full well I'm not racist, but

Aboriginal people have an unfair advantage over the rest of us."

"Yeah, with their high poverty levels and low life expectancy, who wouldn't be jealous of their advantages?" Carol needed a break. "I'm taking my lunch break. Going to check out that new sushi place. Do you want me to bring you back some?"

"Sushi? That Asian muck? No. Pick me up some fish and chips on your way back."

While Carol took a few precious moments of quiet and reflected on the life choices that got her into this awful job, Paula was left alone to think.

Paula, dear Reader, should never be left alone to think. She formulated an outrageous plan. She was going to climb that rock. She was going to have Carol call all the media outlets to witness the event. Had Carol been there and not waiting in line for a couple of chicken teriyaki sushi rolls, she might have pointed out that Paula was middle-aged, unfit, afraid of heights, and had no idea how different the desert was from her air-conditioned city office.

Unfortunately, Carol was not there, and Pauline solidified her plan with an iron will, which would not later be changed.

The day came. The red desert was unbelievably hot. Carol urged Paula to take a water bottle on her climb. Paula told her she could carry it, since she was climbing too. Carol looked at the Rock. She looked at the indigenous people quietly standing in a dignified protest, and the cameras and made a long overdue decision.

She handed Paula the water bottle and said, "I quit." She walked over to the protesters, and stood silently beside them.

Paula started to climb. After the first ten steps, she knew she'd made a mistake. After twenty steps up the sharply-angled rock face, she started to wonder if there was a way to back out of this without losing face. At twenty-five steps, she looked around, was horrified at how high she was, and yet how little of the distance she'd traversed.

She froze. She started to cry. She struggled to breathe.

Sitting down, she looked back over the gathered journalists and camera people, the indigenous protest, and Carol, standing, watching her make a fool of herself.

Well, she would not give up. She would show them all. Practically crawling, she went on a little further, and fell down a crack in the rock.

Indigenous rangers would fail to find her, because she wasn't there.

Paula landed in a very strange place. Animals were speaking, not in a sensible language like English, but some garbled sound she didn't understand. Two groups of giant snakes appeared to be fighting each other. One tail hit her and sent her flying to another place on the rock, where kangaroos or wallabies or something similar were sitting around a campfire, talking in the strange language. A lizard moved languidly from under the shade of an overhang, and spoke to her in what might have been that same language that she didn't understand.

So, dear Reader, we leave Paula in her new home. At least she's safe from all those horrible people who disagree with her opinions, or at least people who disagree with her in English.

Bloody Mary

Settle in dear Reader, while I tell you the strange tale of Rachael, who made fun of people who believed in things she thought weren't real.

Rachael was a relatively successful social media influencer. Her brand was all about disparaging people's beliefs. It didn't matter if it was a religious belief, a belief in ghosts or other supernatural beings, aliens or big foot, or belief in urban legends. If people expressed a belief in anything which could not be empirically measured, documented, proven and re-proven, Rachael would make fun of them for likes and money.

If people took offence at anything she said, she had mastered the art of even making their complaints look foolish.

When one critic challenged her to test out the Bloody Mary myth, by standing in front of a mirror and reciting "Bloody Mary" three times, Rachael accepted the challenge.

They say pride goes before a fall, dear Reader, and Rachael was proud, and condescending, and self-absorbed. For two weeks she promised she was going to prove once and for all that this urban legend was untrue. She boasted that she was going to do a live feed of her experiment. Her followers egged her on and promised to watch.

The day came. She had set up a camera in her bathroom, aimed at the mirror.

"Hello everyone," she said to the camera as the live feed began. "Two weeks ago Henry257 challenged me to disprove the Bloody Mary urban legend. The legend goes that if you look in a mirror and say Bloody Mary three times, she will appear.

"There's been a really bad movie made about this myth, and it even made it to an episode of a popular tv series about supernatural things. Despite it being it being so well known, like all urban legends, it's still shrouded in confusion and contradictions.

"Exactly who Mary is varies with different versions of the story. There's a lot of criminal Marys in history. What she'll do when she appears is also up for debate and wild speculation. This is related to another stupid superstition that mirrors are portals to some other place or dimension, or well, again, it's vague.

"Any person with any shred of common sense will already know what the result of this experiment is going to be. Let's do this, and get it over with, so we can all laugh at Henry257 and everyone else who believes in this stupid urban myth."

Rachael faced the mirror, with her back to the camera. She held up a fist, so it could be clearly seen on the camera, and said, "Bloody Mary." She held up one finger.

She said, "Bloody Mary," a second time, and held up a second finger.

When she said "Bloody Mary" a third time, hands and arms dripping with a black oozing goo reached out from the mirror, grabbed Rachael's head and pulled her into the mirror.

Her horrified viewers typed things like: "What's going on?" and "Rachael, are you all right?" and "Rachael, what happened?"

They didn't receive any answers.

So dear Reader, Rachael is no longer available on social media. I've heard, however, (from a friend of a friend whose cousin's neighbour tried it) if you say "Condescending Rachael" three times in a mirror, she'll appear, call you an idiot and tell you why everything you believe in is a lie.

Busybody

Settle in, dear Reader, while I tell you the strange tale of Agnes, who loved to mind everyone else's business, but learned not everyone puts up with busybodies.

At sixty-five, Agnes finally retired from her factory job, sold the house she'd inherited from her parents, which was too big for her, and moved to a flat in the city. The block of flats had a courtyard in the middle, so she could look out of her windows to see the windows of other flats in the building.

Being bored, and liking to know everyone else's business, Agnes spent a great deal of her day looking out of her windows, into whatever neighbours' windows were within her range of vision and didn't have heavy curtains.

On the same floor as her, on the opposite side of the courtyard, directly opposite her lounge room, there was a window which was especially interesting. It was the bedroom of a young woman in her twenties. Agnes did not approve of young women living on their own. They ought to be home with their families, she believed.

This particular young woman had her bedroom decorated various shades of a pinky-purple colour. The curtains were gauzy and easy to look right through. Agnes thought it was obvious a young woman who would live in a flat on her own in the city would be an exhibitionist. Beside that window was the girl's lounge room, which Agnes could easily watch from her own bedroom.

The girl seemed to be a student, at least she seemed to spend a lot of time working on a computer. She frequently had take-away food delivered, too lazy to cook of course. Young people were lazy these days. Some days, the girl went out for several hours. Agnes noted the days were regular, Mondays, Tuesdays and Fridays. The girl spent ages to get ready to go out on these days, pulling several outfits from the wardrobe

38

before choosing one, putting on make-up and doing her hair carefully. Perhaps she had lectures on those days, or she was running around with boys. That was more likely, Agnes concluded. Young girls on their own would run around with boys. Agnes had never seen a boy in the girl's flat, but she knew what young people were like. That would be why she took so much trouble with her appearance on those days. And where did a girl get money to rent a flat like that anyway? Agnes was sure she was up to something.

Perhaps, dear Reader, if Agnes had found something interesting to fill her own life instead of spying on someone else's she might have avoided what came next.

Agnes had fallen asleep in her recliner in the lounge room, she'd been watching the girl read in bed, trying to make out the book cover. She was certain it was some kind of racy, awful, piece of trash. That was what young girls read if they weren't supervised.

Agnes woke with a start. She had heard something, something which she could only describe as a whimper. Getting up, Agnes went to the window to look in the neighbour's windows. There was still a faint light from the reading lamp in the girl's bedroom. Agnes could see a silhouette of someone wearing a top hat and cloak. What kind of costume was that to be wearing? And why did the girl have someone in her room at this time of night? The girl was lying on the bed, still and silent.

The figure in the top hat turned to look out the window. In moonlight and the light from the room, Agnes could make out a man with sharp features and black eyes. He looked directly at her, his black eyes locked on to her pale blue ones.

Agnes couldn't believe what happened next, the man jumped out of the window, but instead of falling to the ground, seemed to fold up, the cloak stretching out, becoming the wings of a bat. Agnes was frozen in shock, as the bat flew straight across the courtyard and in through her window. In a moment the bat unfolded into the tall man, who grabbed her by the shoulders and pulled her in close, sinking his teeth into her neck.

So, dear Reader, we leave Agnes, who died because she didn't mind her own business. Won't she be surprised when she discovers that death is just the beginning of her problems?

Fog

Settle in dear Reader, while I tell you the strange tale of Carmel, who loved bushwalking, sadly, she didn't love taking expert advice.

Carmel loved bushwalking. It was her favourite pastime. When she had the opportunity to buy a house adjacent an rainforested national park, she jumped at the chance.

The day after moving, she put on her walking shoes and went next door, to the park. At the entrance she saw a notice which said: "Do not enter this national park during fog. If fog arises while you are in the park, do not move. Stay in position and wait for the fog to clear."

She'd never seen a sign like that before, and she'd visited a lot of national parks.

The park was a large one, large enough to have an actual ranger station and amenities a couple of hundred metres in from the front gate. Beside those was a camping area, with electric barbecues. No open fires here.

Carmel decided it would be polite to stop in and introduce herself as a new neighbour, and while there ask about the strange notice near the front gate.

A ranger named Charlie advised her there were eight rangers rostered on at different times, partly to manage the park, but also because someone had to be available to patrol the camping ground. Charlie told her very dense fogs were a regular occurrence in the forest. "The fog comes up during the night, or sometimes late afternoon. It's dangerous, people get disoriented, get lost. Sometimes we don't find them for months. If the fog comes up while you're walking, it's serious. Just accept you're probably staying there until late morning when the sun burns the fog off. Don't think you can follow the path. We've found enough bodies to know it can't be done."

Charlie seemed serious. Carmel, an experienced bushwalker, wondered if perhaps the bodies they'd found were people who didn't know the bush at all well, foreign tourists, probably.

Over the next few months, Carmel made a habit of walking one of the park's many bushwalking tracks after work each day. On weekends she walked the longer tracks, taking her lunch and water bottle. This was exactly the life she wanted. She'd often say hello to Charlie or one of the other rangers, as she met them along the track.

Occasionally she dropped a home-made cake or biscuits in at the ranger station, because she did appreciate how well-maintained the park, and particularly the walking paths, were.

At night, Carmel could look out her window, and see the fog coming in, not as far as the camping area and ranger station, but covering most of the deeper parts of the rainforest.

As the year moved toward winter, the fog came up earlier and earlier in the evening.

On Saturday morning in late May, with winter just around the corner, Carmel packed her backpack with sandwiches and fruit, and her water bottle. It already contained a first aid kit and a silver emergency blanket, not that she thought she'd ever need them.

When she arrived at the park, the fog was just lifting. Not only was it arriving earlier, it was leaving later. She said hello to Charlie, who was repairing a picnic table, as she walked past.

"Don't stay out late," he told her. "Fog's coming in early now."

"I'll be back in time," she answered, and she really did intend to be back well before dark.

Wasn't there a saying, dear Reader, about a road paved with good intentions?

Carmel walked four hours along the path to her favourite waterfall. She sat on a big flat rock in the middle of the shallow creek, with sparkling trickles of water rushing around her and over the edge of a cliff face. She ate her lunch and packed her food away.

The warm, but not too hot, late autumn sun, and the bubbling sound of the water running and falling, made her feel sleepy. Carmel stretched out on the rock for a short nap.

When she woke up, the sun didn't seem to be up quite so high. Carmel looked at her watch. It was three in the afternoon. With four hours to walk back she wouldn't be at the park entrance until seven. Could she cut that time?

Half walking, half running, Carmel followed the track back. Hurrying took all her energy, and soon she was too tired to do more than her normal walk.

After a while she stopped for a drink, finishing the last of what was in her water bottle. She looked at her watch. It was four-thirty. Looking around, she realised she was almost halfway back.

She picked up her bag and set out again. It was around five-thirty when the trees started to look out-of-focus, and the air began to feel damp. The fog was coming in, but she still had reasonable visibility, so she continued walking.

The fog thickened quickly. Soon she couldn't see more than a metre in front of her face. She gave in and decided she would have to wait until morning. Feeling uncomfortable in the clinging damp, Carmel pulled the emergency blanket out of the backpack and wrapped it around herself. She sat down, and propped herself, and her backpack up against an ancient tree right beside the path. Searching the bag, she found she still had an apple, which she ate, deciding it was dinner.

She pulled out her phone, thinking she would call the ranger station and let them know she was spending the night out on the path. The phone had no signal, which was strange. Previously, she'd been able to find a signal anywhere in the park.

With nothing else to do, Carmel decided to go to sleep, even though she was not in a comfortable position. She napped fitfully for a while, then was pulled to full wakefulness with a sudden jolt. She'd heard a noise, not the usual rustlings in the underbrush and birdcalls in the canopy she expected in the rainforest. She was sure what she'd heard had been human.

The sound came again. It was definitely human; a woman, calling for help. Then she heard a man yelling. The woman's voice called again.

Carmel was fairly certain she could tell what direction the sounds were coming from. "Hold on! I'm coming!" she yelled.

Leaving the backpack behind, Carmel took the first aid kit and her phone, which she used as a torch to try to see through the fog. After a few steps she dropped the emergency blanket which she'd been wearing like a cloak.

So, dear Reader, that's where we leave Carmel. In the morning the rangers will find her backpack and the emergency blanket. A search party will be called which will find her phone and first aid kit. In two months' time, rangers will find what's left of her body. Her essence, her soul, that part which makes Carmel herself, well: if you go bushwalking in the fog, you might hear that part calling out to you for help, among the other voices of the lost.

Designer

Settle in, dear Reader, while I tell you the strange tale of Adelaide, who made her living doing something she loved, but who dreamed of greater success.

Adelaide made dresses, not ordinary dresses, but beautiful, amazing, incredible dresses, the kind of dresses that always drew attention.

She made the kind of dresses that were too special, too impractical, and too uncomfortable, for everyday use.

Adelaide made dresses for weddings, balls, high school formals, and dance students. All of her creations were of her own design from start to finish. While talking with the client about what they wanted and the event, she would draw the dress. The drawing would incorporate the client's ideas, but it was all Adelaide's imagination. As she drew, she chose colours and shaped the dress to flatter the client.

No matter the clients' age or shape or personal assets, she would look stunning in a dress made by Adelaide.

Everyone in her small town knew if you wanted a dress for a very special occasion you went to Adelaide. Women and girls ordered their gowns months in advance, afraid of missing out.

Unlike many people working in creative industries, Adelaide had a steady stream of clients, and made a reasonable living. She loved her work, loved everything from the texture of the fabrics, to the design work, to the delight on her clients' faces when they collected their perfect dresses made especially for them.

You might think, dear Reader, that Adelaide was living the perfect life, earning a living from doing what she loved to do. Adelaide however, was not happy. She was jealous of famous designers whose clients walked catwalks and red carpets and had endless attention. Adelaide was the best dressmaker in her town, but she wanted to dress stars, not local brides and girls going to formals. She was sure she would be happy if she designed and made clothes for the rich and famous.

Sometimes, small town fame leads to something more widespread.

One of those high school girls who had been so excited to have a formal dress made by Adelaide, went on to fame and fortune as a singer.

When Melissa Carr made the big time, there was only one person she wanted making her clothes. Adelaide was sewing for a star, making costumes for video clips and concerts, for awards shows and all of the glitzy places a star had to go.

Adelaide was sewing day and night, for just one client, referring everyone else to other dressmakers in town, whose work was not the same standard as hers.

Melissa bragged about her exclusive dressmaker to others in her circle, and soon Adelaide was sewing for even more famous people. She had to hire an assistant, and then two assistants.

Adelaide began to imagine herself leading a business rivalling Chanel, Dior or other haute couture design houses.

Her assistants, however, did not have the same attention to detail as Adelaide. They didn't have her skill, so she still did most of the work herself.

Orders poured in, and she was sleeping fewer and fewer hours, trying to meet the unrealistic deadlines of clients who were far more demanding than any she'd previously had.

Any work she trusted to assistants had to be checked, and often re-done, so even the help seemed worse than unhelpful.

The day came, when she missed her deadline. The client in question simply wore another gown, provided by a more famous designer.

That client never ordered anything else from Adelaide.

Over the next few weeks, she missed more deadlines, and lost more clients.

Then, the assistants came to work and found Adelaide sitting on the floor, crying uncontrollably over a lace skirt she was beading, while shaking wildly. A visit to the doctor resulted in Adelaide being ordered to rest for at least a fortnight, or risk having to be admitted to hospital.

A fortnight is a long time in the world of what's popular at the moment. It was long enough for all of her famous clients, apart from Melissa, to forget her.

And so dear Reader, we leave Adelaide, who has learned to be happy sewing for the special events in the lives of the women of her local community, with the occasional special dress for her one remaining famous client, who always asks if Adelaide's very sure she has time.

Eternal Spring

Settle in dear Reader, while I tell you the strange tale of Kristen, who had a wish come true, and lived to regret it.

It was one of those glorious October days. The Brisbane sky was that special, glorious, intense, blue it only wears in spring.

Kristen looked up through the branches of the jacaranda tree in her back yard. The vibrant purple flowers had erupted and were taking over the tree, preparatory to lightly falling and creating the purple carpet which covers so much of the city as spring progresses.

This was her favourite time of the year, the time when her home city was most beautiful, when she most loved where she lived.

She looked at the tapestry of purple flowers and green leaves against the blue sky. The colours were alive, intense, and seemed so perfect. Kristen let out a deep sigh.

"I wish," she said quietly, "spring would last for ever. I wish the jacaranda bloomed all year round, that the sky was always this clear and blue, that the weather was this fine. I wish every day was like today."

Words spoken to empty air, words that no-one hears don't have any effect, do they, dear Reader? Yet, so many ancient cultures believed trees had spirits. From the Greek Dryads, to the Gallic Druantia, to the Baltic Lauma, to the Phillipine Anito, to the Madagascan Rakapila, to the Chinese Pi-Fang to the malevolent Indian Yashinis, people around the world believed trees had powerful spirits. Of course, we know better than that now, don't we?

Something heard her wish. Surely not a tree spirit, because we know those aren't real, but *something* did.

The next day was just as clear and beautiful as that one, as was the next and the next.

By December, when spring ought to have begun to move into summer, it was obvious something was not right.

The flowers never left the jacarandas. The annual purple carpet never happened.

The flame trees which usually exploded in bright red flowers, taking over from the jacarandas, heralding the shift from spring to summer, and decorating the city for Christmas, never came.

December moved into January.

January didn't bring the summer rains. No clouds disturbed the beautiful clear blue sky.

Water restrictions were placed.

Gardens died, but the big trees, like the jacarandas were able to withstand the drought.

Fruit trees failed to receive the signals of temperature change and rain, and did not form flowers or fruit.

Vegetable growers saw their crops die in the field for lack of rain.

What should have been summer wore on, with no rain, just unrelenting blue skies, and purple flowers who lived long past their appointed time.

No-one missed the heat and humidity of summer, but everyone missed the water from the rain. Even Kristen began to resent the rich beautiful flowers of the jacaranda.

Kristen stood under the tree, hating the flowers she'd loved so much. "What happened? Why can't the weather be normal? I just want everything the way it should be," she cried.

Out of the clear sky, a large lightning bolt struck the tree beside her, the explosive "bang" of thunder felt as though it went through her entire body.

Clouds came rushing from everywhere and nowhere, and the sky turned black.

The rain began, and did not stop. It was like a raging animal, as it drenched and drowned the parched landscape. Suburbs flooded, but the rain did not stop.

A whole summer's rain fell in days.

Then the sky cleared. The weather went back to normal.

The jacaranda in Kristen's yard never recovered, but stood scorched as a permanent reminder of an unending spring.

And so, dear Reader, we leave Kristen who will always be more careful of her words. Words, after all, have the power to change the world.

Plants

Settle in dear Reader, while I tell you the strange tale of Sharon, who wanted to do something different with her life, but never realised how different it could be.

Sharon worked six days a week as a supermarket cashier, but still struggled to pay her rent.

She lived frugally, picked up extra shifts, and worked the longest hours she could, but always found that at the end of the pay there was too much fortnight left.

In the break room one day, while she ate her sandwiches, she flicked through a magazine, that had been removed from the store because it was damaged.

There was an ad looking for a housekeeper for a remote scientific facility. Accommodation was provided, and the wage was far better than the supermarket paid her.

With nothing to lose, and seemingly everything to gain, Sharon applied.

Sharon got the job, of course, and travelled to central western Queensland, to a facility on a dirt track near Boulia. Her old car rattled and shook along the dirt track, but it got her safely there.

She was surprised, having expected a fancy gleaming science-y building, to find a ramshackle old Queenslander, on high blocks, with the downstairs enclosed with concrete blocks. Behind the house was a huge greenhouse.

At the front door she was greeted by a man who looked like a scientist stereotype, and she couldn't help but think of Doc from the Back to the Future movies.

He introduced himself as Dr Evan Evans, and said his assistant Peter, had gone into town for supplies.

He explained that what they did there was using a combination of cross breeding and genetic modification, to produce experimental plants which would eventually lead to the crops that would feed the world in the future.

She would live in the house, along with Dr Evans and Peter, and would be responsible for cleaning the house and preparing all of the meals. She would not be required in the lab under the house, but would occasionally have to help out in the greenhouse if the others were away.

At that point, a man arrived, and began to unload groceries from the back of a once-white-now-dirt-coloured van.

Sharon rushed to help She introduced herself to Peter. Like Sharon, he was in his mid-twenties, and would tell her over coffee later that he was a PhD student, supervised by Dr Evans.

Dr Evans suggested Peter show Sharon how to attend to the plants in the glasshouse when he went that afternoon.

Outside the glasshouse, Peter hit a yellow button beside the door. Through the misted glass, Sharon could see water raining down inside.

"We water for ten minutes before entering," Peter said. "These are all experimental plants, some of which are ferns and mushrooms that give off spores. Watering before we enter ensure there's no floating spores in the air that might escape. We don't know what these plants would do in the environment, so we can't take chances."

Sharon nodded.

Peter continued, "While the plants are being watered we grab a bag of plant food."

He opened a door to the side of the door to the lab. There was a room filled with filled sacks, along with a wheelbarrow and a couple of shovels.

Lifting a sack into the wheelbarrow, Peter said, "Can you grab the shovels?"

"Sure," she said, picking up the two shovels.

As they arrived back at the glasshouse, the water stopped running, and there was a buzzing noise. The door clicked.

Peter pulled the door open and pushed the wheelbarrow through.

There was something very off putting about the plants, Sharon found. Perhaps it was because she'd never seen plants that looked anything like them before. More likely it was because they appeared to have eyes and teeth.

Peter looked at her confused expression and laughed. "The Doc Evans' sense of humour," he explained. "He breeds them to look like they've got faces. Don't worry. It's just an illusion."

He used a sharp edge if the shovel to cut open the side of the sack. There was an overpowering smell.

"Blood and bone fertiliser. These experimental plants need a good feeding twice a week. We do Monday and Thursday. We just shovel it out and spread it evenly between them all. Then we get the second sack. Two sacks, spread evenly feed the whole lot."

"I'm not a scientist, of course," Sharon said, "but it seems strange to me that the plants that are going to solve world hunger shouldn't need an animal-based fertiliser twice a week, especially so much of it."

Peter laughed again. Sharon decided she liked the sound of his laugh. "Well I am a scientist, and it only makes sense to me because I know these aren't the final product. They're just a stage in development. We're developing principles, finding out what works and doesn't. It's all very experimental at the moment. You're right. Nothing that depends on animal products is ever going to feed the planet's growing population."

Sharon settled in to her new routine. The work was not hard, and at night she, Peter and Dr Evans would often play cards or board games, as telephone, internet and television reception were all very patchy.

Most days, she would go for a walk around the property, and walking along a quiet little creek, not far from the house. Once a week, she or Peter would go to town for supplies, and while there she would use the precious telephone signal to call family or friends, or order books and other items online. All in all, she felt her new life was a great improvement on the one she had left behind.

When something seems too good to be true, dear Reader, it's frequently either not true, not good, or not either.

It was a Thursday afternoon and Sharon was starting to prepare dinner. She turned on a tap, instead of the regular flow of water, there were gurgling and grunting noises and the tiniest trickle.

Sharon pressed the button for the intercom to the lab and told Dr Evans about the problem. He said he would fix it.

Looking out the window, moments later, she saw Dr Evans with a large spanner working on the pipes coming from the water tanks.

Then he called her on the intercom and said the primary water tank had run out and he'd just changed over to the secondary tank. He said if they didn't get rain soon, they would need a water carter to fill the tanks.

Sharon absorbed this information, for the first time realising how precarious life outside of the city really was.

Dr Evans came upstairs for dinner, but Peter did not.

"He's working late, you can put his dinner in the fridge for later," Dr Evans said.

Sharon did so. By the time she went for bed, Peter had not returned.

The next morning, he was still absent.

"Peter decided to leave. He's abandoned his studies," Dr Evans said.

"How did he leave? His van's still here?" Sharon was genuinely puzzled.

"Oh the van is mine. Peter was just driving it while he was here. A friend of his came to pick him up last night. You were asleep, and he didn't want to wake you to say good bye. Until I have another assistant, you will have to take over feeding the plants."

Life continued on, almost as usual until Monday, when Sharon went to feed the plants. She hit the sprinklers, and went to load up the wheelbarrow.

After the door clicked open, Sharon wheeled the loaded barrow in, broke open the sack the way she'd seen Peter do, and began to spread the stinking fertiliser.

She saw something glint in the wet dirt and fertiliser slurry on the glasshouse floor. Picking it up, she saw it was a man's watch. She turned it over to see engraved on the back: "For Peter on your twenty-first birthday, love Mum and Dad."

Why would Peter drop his watch in here and not pick it up? It obviously had sentimental value.

She tucked the mucky watch into her jeans pocket, planning to ask Dr Evans if he had a forwarding address for Peter.

Sandra went back to re-load the wheelbarrow. Dr Evans was there.

"You have to do it faster," he said. "You have to spread all of the fertiliser and be out of the greenhouse before the plants dry."

"I'm working as fast as I can," Sandra answered. "You can help if you want to make it faster."

He didn't follow her through the door, but stood outside and watched her work.

That seemed strange. If the job had to be done so quickly, and the scientist had time to stand in the doorway, surely he could help.

She spread fertiliser as quickly as she could.

Suddenly, she saw a movement. She jumped back a step. One of the plants had definitely moved. Then another. Those mouths that were just an illusion were presenting a very good illusion of opening, of baring teeth. Stems stretched toward her.

She ran for the door, to see the Doctor starting to close it.

She pushed against the door and fought her way out.

"What the hell was that?" she demanded.

"Nothing. There's nothing, just plants."

"Just plants! If it's just plants, you go in there!"

"You can't tell anyone! My research will be over!"

"It bloody well should be!"

The doctor tried to grab Sandra by the throat.

She jumped back, out of his reach. Realising she was still holding a shovel, she used it to hit him in the head.

The scientist collapsed in the doorway.

Sharon put all her weight against the door, pushing it closed, pushing Dr Evans along with it, and locking him in.

He must have recovered consciousness, as she heard screams. She couldn't open the door to help him. The door would only unlock after the sprinklers had run for ten minutes, even if, as on the previous feeding day, very little water had run through them.

And so, dear Reader, we leave Sharon, heading in to town with a story to tell, and with a future back in the city, standing at the checkout and glad for the challenges of the life she leads.

Housekeeper

Settle in dear Reader, while I tell you the strange tale of Miranda, who just wanted a little help around the house, but discovered being an early adopter of technology had issues.

Miranda was watching tv after a busy day at work. She was exhausted, and trying to avoid looking at the work that needed to be done around her house.

That was when she saw the ad. AI Tech, a new startup was selling robot assistants. They looked human and could be programmed for any number of tasks.

In her lunch break the next day, she went to the new AI Tech shop, to ask about a housekeeper.

The salesman showed her a doll, the size of a human adult. "She's made of steel, covered with a silky soft plastic to mimic human skin. Her brain is the most advanced artificial intelligence available now. Once you order your robot, we can program her for whatever your needs are. Since you want a housekeeper, we'll give her our housekeeping program. Compared to the cost of hiring a human housekeeper, she will pay for herself in less than a year. We have an easy payment plan, and of course, if she malfunctions in that first year, you are able to return her as long as there's no user-caused damage."

Miranda chose her robot, giving skin, hair and eye colour choice, and explaining the household tasks she wanted the robot to do. She chose the name Rosie, thinking of a cartoon robot from her childhood television watching.

After work the next day, she went to collect her new housekeeper.

"She's programmed for housekeeping," the salesman said, "but she can learn. If you want more tasks done, you just have to explain them to her. She knows when her power is running down, and will return herself to her charging station. Anything else you need to know you can find in the manual, or call our helpline number."

As Miranda walked to the car with Rosie by her side, she noticed Rosie walked a little stiffly, but looked human.

"You know, we might want to get you some new clothes, so you don't have to wear that maid's uniform all the time," Miranda said.

"Whatever you say, Madam," Rosie answered.

"You can call me Miranda."

"Yes, Miranda."

At home, Rosie went straight to work, cleaning the house, sweeping, mopping dusting. She washed Miranda's clothes, made the bed, then cleaned the kitchen. Miranda has nothing to do but rest, while Rosie then cooked her dinner.

Things are looking good at the moment, dear Reader, but remember early adopters of technology often find there are glitches.

That night, Miranda was woken by the sound of the vacuum. She explained to Rosie that cleaning during the night wasn't necessary.

The next morning, Rosie made breakfast for Miranda, and cleaned the kitchen while Miranda ate.

That afternoon, Miranda found the furniture polished to the point of gleaming. Dinner was cooked, and there were fresh baked bread and biscuits.

After the dishes were done, Miranda told Rosie to stop working for the night.

"What should Rosie do?" The robot asked.

"Ah, what do you do when you're not working, recharge, relax, whatever."

"Rosie does not need to be recharged."

"Oh, OK, then just relax."

"What is relax?"

"Ah, shut down until morning. That's it, shut down until six am."

"Shutting down."

Rosie simply stopped moving and stood silently in the middle of the lounge room. Miranda found it unnerving.

Another morning came, and while Miranda appreciated her home being cleaned, and meals prepared. She noticed the pattern on her plate seemed worn thin. This was quite new china.

"Rosie, how often do you wash the dishes?"

"Ten times per day."

"They don't get dirtied ten times per day."

"Rosie cleans until told to stop cleaning."

"You need more to do. Perhaps you could mow the lawn or weed the garden."

"Rosie will download instructions on how to do those things."

Miranda came home to find her lawn mowed, her plants pruned and garden beds weeded. Perhaps all she'd really needed to do was keep Rosie busy.

Inside the house was clean, and Rosie was cooking dinner.

"The yard looks nice. Did you have enough to do today, Rosie?" Miranda asked.

"Rosie had enough to do."

"Oh, good," Miranda said.

When she went for her shower that night, she noticed worn areas in the enamel of the bath. How many times did a bath have to be scrubbed before the enamel began to wear out?

Was there more work she could give Rosie? Was there a way to stop Rosie working when the work was done?

After her shower, Miranda read and re-read the manual. It didn't say anything about a robot continuing to work even though there was no work left to do. She would call the help line when she got home the next day.

Rosie made breakfast and was already vacuuming while Miranda ate.

When Miranda got home from work, her lawn had been mowed so short there were bare patches, and the plants had been pruned down to bare stems.

Miranda called the help line. She explained the problem.

The help desk person said: "Your robot was programmed for working in large hotels or university residential colleges. It's really not suitable for the home."

"Then why was it sold to me for home use?"

"That's the retailer, AI Tech. I work for the developer, Technical AI."

"So what do I do?"

"I can't tell you what to do. But you don't have enough work for your robot."

"Thank you."

The next day, Miranda returned Rosie to the store, and cancelled her payment plan.

It turned out she could not hire a housekeeper for the amount she had been paying for Rosie, but she could hire a cleaner to come once a week, which was a great help.

So, dear Reader, Miranda is much happier now. She has help around the house, so the housework isn't so onerous, and she's decided she's not going to be the first to adopt new technology in future.

Nose

Settle in dear Reader, while I tell you the strange tale of Carla, who always felt insecure despite being both very smart and kind.

At work, Carla's manager always took credit for her work with the higher-ups. She never complained, never agitated for promotion, just efficiently did her work, which Ed would take credit for.

After work each day, she went to her grandmother's house, cooked her grandmother's dinner, did whatever housework was needed and stayed to talk, or mostly listen.

Then she went home to her single-bedroom flat, exhausted, to read a book for a while, and sleep.

At weekends she cleaned her mother's house as well as her own, but still cooked her grandmother's dinner.

Sometimes, she would find the time to go to a movie alone, or to the library.

It was a busy life, with little social interaction outside her family, but she didn't even stop to wonder if she wanted more.

One afternoon, her grandmother, Agnes, said, "I am sick. I went to the doctor yesterday, no don't worry, I didn't go alone. I decided it was time someone else helped me out instead of dumping everything on you and I demanded your aunt take me. She doesn't work and she has the time. The doctor says I'm circling the drain. Since Valerie knew yesterday, the rest of the family will know by now. The vultures are going to start gathering to pick over my bones. Oh sweetie, don't cry. Before they start going through my things, I want you to have one particular thing. Under my bed there's a box, go and get it, and I'll tell you about it."

Obediently, and with tears running down her face, Carla got the box. She brought it back and opened it, and was confused by the contents. It was a very old clown costume, complete with a red nose.

Grandma Agnes said, "The two people in my life who have been kindest to me were my father and you. This was my father's costume when he was performing. He was billed as a clown, but he was also a magician, and he did the most amazing tricks, making them all look like accidents. The audience was always amazed and never sure they'd seen what they had. After he died, I used to carry that red nose around in my pocket. Whenever I felt insecure, or sad or frightened, I would squeeze that nose. Under the costume, there's a scrap book, with all of the press clippings about Marvello the Clown. This is an important part of my life, and some of my favourite memories. I want you to have it."

The tears were flowing freely now, and through the sniffs and tears, Carla said, "Grandma, I don't know what to say."

"You don't have to say anything. Your actions speak far louder than any words ever could. For years, none of the family has come to see me unless I have called. You just come every day, unasked. I'm sure no-one else knows how I get my groceries, or have my meals cooked or my house cleaned, and they don't care enough to ask. I know you don't tell anyone what you do for me. I'll bet at your work you don't get credit for what you do. So now, I want you to put that red nose in your pocket, and give it a squeeze when you are feeling insecure or anxious, but especially when someone is overlooking you or taking credit for something you have done. You are too polite, too kind and too good to get the attention you deserve. Give that nose a squeeze and think of my father who no one could ever overlook, and remember that is your heritage. And when you no longer have me to look after, go and have some fun. Don't let the family fill your time with other work that some of them could be doing."

So, dear Reader, Carla spent her reading time that night reading about the amazing feats of the great grandfather she never knew, discovering his act included not only magic that other magicians openly declared was too advanced for them, incredible feats of acrobatics, and slapstick. She began to wish she had known this amazing man, and could imagine Grandma Agnes as a little girl watching him on the stage, utterly enraptured.

The next morning at work, Ed had her print up multiple copies of quarterly sales reports she had compiled and already sent to him electronically, and bring them to the board room.

She walked into the room with the stack of papers, to find Ed in a meeting with the entire executive, from the CEO on down.

At Ed's request she placed a copy of the report in front of each of the men at the table. For the first time it struck her that they were all middle aged white men. The company's official commitment to diversity apparently stopped at the lowest levels of the workplace.

"Once the girl's finished handing the reports out, I'll explain the detail," Ed said to the gathered room.

Following her grandmother's request, she had the red nose in her pocket. She squeezed it, the condescension and the presence of all these old men who had so much power over her had definitely caused her anxiety to skyrocket.

As soon as she'd squeezed the nose, Ed got up from his place, picked up a piece of cake from the refreshments trolley walked over to the CEO and squashed the cake into his face.

The CEO got up, yelled for security, and had Ed escorted from the building.

Carla grabbed serviettes from the refreshments trolley for the CEO to wipe cake and icing from his face.

Then she said, "If you have questions about the report, I can answer them. I compiled it."

"You did?" the CEO asked.

"I've been compiling them for the past five years, along with all of the other work coming out of Ed's office. He spends his days playing games on a hand-held console."

Where had she found the audacity to say that? Was it just the reassurance her grandmother had talked about, from having the nose to squeeze?

By the end of the day, Ed had most definitely been fired, and Carla had been promoted to take his job. A woman in middle management, score one for inclusion.

After work, Carla was keen to tell her grandmother about her promotion.

At her grandmother's house, she found both her mother and her aunt Valerie.

She greeted everyone and went to the kitchen to start cooking her grandmother's dinner. Valerie followed her to the kitchen.

"What are you doing here?" Valerie asked. "You can't just turn up here to try to get something out of her now you know she's dying. Her will's already been made, everything goes to her own children, not her grandchild."

Carla hated confrontation and squeezed the red nose for reassurance. She answered, "I'm not trying to get anything out of her. I come here every day to cook and clean. Why are you here? I've never seen you here before, and even now, I don't see you helping with the work. Who do you think has been looking after Grandma? Did you even care if anyone was? Your kids are grown up and you're still a stay at home mother. Maybe you could try to be less selfish?"

How could she say that to her aunt? Carla expected Valerie to yell at her.

Instead, Valerie crumbled. "I'm sorry. I didn't realise. I didn't even think. Thank you for looking after her. How can I help?"

At Carla's request, Valerie did the washing.

Carla served her grandmother's dinner.

"How dare you interrupt our conversation?" Carla's mother said.

Carla didn't need to squeeze the nose. Grandma Agnes was fierce. "How dare she? How dare you, Charmaine? Carla comes here every day to look after me, and what do you do? I suspect she does your housework as well. She's not a slave, although you seem to think she is. She's an intelligent young woman, who deserves far better than she has from you or any other member of the family, and she's the only one to even think about making sure I have everything I need. Don't you dare criticise her for looking after me. You're both a useless daughter and a useless mother."

Carla was amazed. She'd never seen her sweet grandmother so incredibly angry.

Her mother, in stunned silence, looked from Agnes to Carla and back again. Eventually she said, "I just always thought you had meals on wheels or something. Those things for old people."

"You assumed. You didn't ask. You didn't offer to help me apply for any of those things. For years, you let your daughter work constantly, and never questioned it. Of course, I also let her do all that work, because, selfishly, I wanted her company, because no other family members ever visited me. We've all done Carla a great disservice."

Carla was crying again. "No Grandma, I wanted to do it all for you. I wanted you to be happy."

Agnes smiled at her, "I have been happy. And if I'm not mistaken, you have news to make me even happier and even more proud of you if that were possible."

Carla sniffed, and told her mother and grandmother about her promotion.

That evening, Carla parked her car in her usual spot and walked towards her flat. A man approached her, and she saw he was holding a knife, and was between her and her front door. Carla squeezed the nose, and astonished both herself and the man by doing a triple somersault from a standing position over the man's head, and ran to her flat, unlocked the door and was inside before the man was able to turn to follow.

Carla sat the nose on her dining table, and on her laptop searched for magical objects.

So, dear Reader, Carla learned of talismans, small magical objects, imbued with magical powers by the belief of the owner. She realised Grandma Agnes had trusted this nose for so many years her faith in it had given it power, power that was now in Carla's own hands, which would grow as Carla trusted it more. Because Grandma had associated it with her father, its powers seemed to be similar to aspects of his stage acts; slapstick, like the cake incident, acrobatics like the incident outside her door that night, the confidence to speak like a stage performer. The only aspect of his stage performance she hadn't yet seen was magic, although the whole thing was magic, wasn't it?

She decided that in future she would only buy clothes with pockets, so she could always keep this talisman close.

After work the next day, she found her mother cooking Agnes' dinner, while Valerie was cleaning the house.

Grandma Agnes asked her to come and sit and talk.

Carla told Agnes about her research.

"Talisman," Grandma Agnes said. "I never knew the word. I just knew what it did. I always thought the magic was my father's. If you saw him on the stage, you would believe the magic was real."

Agnes died that night. When her solicitor revealed that Agnes had given each of her daughters a small amount of money, but the house, all of her most prized possessions, and the bulk of a large amount of money were to go to Carla, there were objections from both Charmaine and Valerie.

Both daughters threatened to take it to court, believing they ought to have everything. The solicitor gave everyone a copy of a letter from Agnes that had accompanied the will, which explained all Carla had done for her and how little her daughters, and other grandchildren, had. The solicitor made it clear this letter would go to the court if either Charmaine or Valerie contested the will. They gave in.

So, dear Reader, Carla no longer has a grandmother, but she has her memories, she is no longer taken for granted at her job, and she has a house of her own, not a tiny rented flat. Are you disappointed dear Reader? Did you expect everything to go wrong for Carla? Sometimes magic doesn't go wrong.

Inheritance

Settle in dear Reader, while I tell you the strange tale of Jane, who received an amazing inheritance, but quickly found it wasn't as good as it sounded.

Jane's mother, Melissa, had never talked about her family, except to say she'd run away as a teenager and was never going back. Whenever Jane asked anything about them, her mother would refuse to answer. Whenever Jane asked anything about her father, Melissa would say he was not worth talking about.

As Jane grew up, all of the other kids she knew would talk about grandparents, or cousins, or aunts or uncles, or even brothers and sisters, and Jane would wonder about her own extended family, who they were, and what was so terrible about them that Melissa would never speak about them. But there was just her mother and her.

When Jane married Kevin, Melissa walked her down the aisle, and did all of the things a father of the bride should do, in addition to all the things a bride's mother should do. Privately, she told Jane, that should she ever need to leave, she was always welcome back in her, Melissa's, home.

Melissa said something similar again, when Jane's daughter, Kirsty, was born. Jane had said, there was no reason she would ever need to leave Kevin.

Melissa had nodded knowingly, and said, "I certainly hope there isn't, but if there ever is, I'm here."

Jane wondered what had happened to her mother that made her so suspicious, so ready to believe things would turn out badly.

Eventually, Melissa was diagnosed with cervical cancer, and her health went downhill quickly. One of the doctors mentioned casually to Jane, how the scarring from so many old injuries had affected surgery and ongoing treatment.

At Melissa's funeral, Jane reflected sadly, that perhaps it was good that Melissa had not suffered for long from the cancer and its treatment, but what had she suffered before that? What had caused such injuries that the aftermath could affect her later medical treatment?

Jane would not wonder for long, dear Reader, as she would soon hear some news that would lead to answers for her life-long questions.

A month after Melissa's death, Jane received a phone call from a solicitor. She was the only living relative, and therefore the heir, for Melissa's father Hubert Greaves, who had died only a week after Melissa had.

Were there no other grandchildren? Jane had asked.

The solicitor hesitated a moment before explaining that even if there had been other grandchildren, she was Hubert Greaves' only surviving child.

Jane was dumbfounded. Did that mean the woman she'd always known as her mother was really her sister?

When the solicitor confirmed that Melissa had been both, Jane began to realise why her mother had fled her family.

Along with a huge amount of money, Jane had inherited a huge amount of house. The house had been extended significantly, it appeared. A part of the ground floor, presumably the original house, had stone walls. A large part of the ground floor, and all of upstairs was brick.

On the day they moved in, Kevin joked about how he would have proposed to Jane much earlier if he'd known how much family money she was getting, and that he wouldn't have to worry about how to earn enough for the family.

Jane pointed out that, apart from a brief maternity leave, she'd always been an equal part of supporting them financially.

She was torn about accepting the family money and the family house, since she had some idea of what "family" had cost her mother.

The first night there, they discovered the electricity was unreliable. Lights would flicker. An old radio suddenly turned itself on in the middle of the night.

Jane began to write a list of things that needed to be done to the house. First on the list was to have an electrician inspect the place and do any needed repairs. Next was to clean up the overgrown gardens. Then there would be a thorough cleaning of the house, and sorting through to decide what could be kept, what would be sold or donated, and what needed to be thrown out.

Exploring the house, she found a room which must have been her mother's. There was a diary on the dressing table. Jane spent an afternoon reading about her mother's life, leading up to the point where, at fourteen, she'd discovered she was pregnant with her abusive father's child, and was planning to run away to protect her baby.

"And now, here I am, back in this house you fled," Jane said quietly.

Kevin called from downstairs. He'd made an odd discovery. "The room sizes in this old part aren't right," he said. "I think there should be another room, but I can't find a door."

They searched the rooms of the old section of the house, there was no way to access an area that seemed to definitely be where a room should be.

Eventually, they went out to the overgrown yard, and found a locked door, in the brick wall, behind trees and overgrown vines. None of the keys they had been given matched the rusted lock on the door. Jane added, "Get locksmith to open secret door" to her list.

That second night, three-year-old Kirsty, insisted on sleeping with Jane and Kevin. She said the girl in her room was crying and keeping her awake.

Kevin checked Kirsty's room. There didn't seem to be anything untoward there, except that it seemed colder than the rest of the house. Strangely, he realised her room would have been directly over the hidden room. He told Jane about his odd realisation when he returned to bed.

Later that night, Jane got up for a drink of water. As she stood by the kitchen sink, she heard the sound of someone crying. She walked toward the wall between the kitchen and the hidden room, and the sound became clearer.

"Hello," Jane called out. "Is there someone there?"

The crying continued.

How could someone be in that room? The lock was rusted. There hadn't been any other entrance. Getting the door opened moved to the top of her list.

When she called the locksmith in the morning, he'd seemed quite abrupt, but he agreed to come first thing.

When he arrived, he said, "I have to tell you my wife was Mr Greave's visiting carer for the last ten years. She wants to know about the family who spent all that time ignoring the poor helpless old man."

"Well, we're a normal family who didn't know he existed, until a lawyer called me," Jane answered. "My mother refused to talk about her family. Maybe the helpless old man your wife knew was different from the younger one my mother ran away from."

The locksmith had the decency to look at least slightly embarrassed. He would go from embarrassed to horrified when he got the door open.

Inside there was a large cage, which had a human skeleton and a couple of old plastic buckets in it.

The police would find another ten skeletons buried in the yard. They would all be found to be teenaged girls, including Melissa's older sister. They had gone missing from the area over many years, starting before Melissa had run away, and continuing on until age and illness had incapacitated Hubert Greaves.

And so, dear, Reader, you will be pleased to know that Jane and her family left that horrible place immediately. When the investigation was complete, the building and garden were bulldozed. Jane gave the land to the city council, to build a park in memory of Hubert Greaves' victims. (Jane would never acknowledge him as her grandfather, and certainly not as her father.) Jane, Kevin and Kirsty are doing well, and have put the horror behind them.

Foretold

Settle in dear Reader, while I tell you the strange tale of Agatha who wanted to know her future, but it didn't turn out as expected.

Agatha had spent her whole life hating the "old woman" name her parents had given her, but had never taken any action to change it.

At fifty-eight years old, with seven years still ahead before retirement, she was starting to feel like the old lady who should have had her name. She was tired all the time. Her work was a constant grind. There didn't seem anything worthwhile in her life.

If asked, she wouldn't have been able to say why she went to the fortune teller. But once we was sitting in the darkened room, the only question she could think to ask was: "When will I die?"

The fortune teller warned her that this was something people should not know.

Agatha insisted.

Madame Karalita (known in her non-working life as Liz Clark) uncovered a crystal ball, and asked the question: "When will Agatha Bourke die?"

Madame's voice was different as she answered herself: "She will die on her sixtieth birthday."

Agatha could see in the ball a grave, with: "Agatha Burke, nineteen sixty-five to twenty twenty-five," written on it.

Whoever had written it hadn't even got her name right! They'd left out the "o" in her last name. It had been spelled B-u-r-k-e instead of B-o-u-r-k-e.

At home that night, Agatha made a decision. Her house had gained value in the thirty years she had owned it. It was now worth a bit over a million dollars. Even in twenty twenty-four, that much money could go a long way. It was a pity her superannuation was locked away until she reached official retirement age.

She made her will, quit her job, and sold her house.

Knowing about her immanent death, gave Agatha a new lease on life. She bought plane tickets and booked hotels, and went on the holiday of a lifetime. Agatha saw all of the many things she'd ever wanted to see. She did all of the things she'd ever wanted to do.

Don't worry, dear Reader, Agatha was careful. She made sure her money would last exactly to her sixtieth birthday, when she'd be back in her home town, and have a massive party with family and friends.

She did that. After two years of a amazing adventures, and feeling young and free for the first time in her life, Agatha booked into a resort hotel in her home town. She invited practically everyone she knew to a dinner in the resort's restaurant the night before her birthday. Everyone had a great time at her expense. Friends wanted to know what adventures she had planned. She shrugged off the questions.

That night, Agatha went to bed in her hotel room, wondering how she would die, whether it would be in her sleep in the early hours of the morning? Would she choke on her breakfast or be hit by a car? Would she drown in the hotel pool?

Morning came and she was still alive. She over-indulged at breakfast, but didn't care since it was her last day alive anyway. After a swim in the hotel pool, she lay in the sun for a while. Who cared about skin cancer now?

Agatha had a very indulgent slow lunch, then went shopping. She would be long gone before the credit card bill was due.

She went to the spa after that, for a massage and a make-over. She planned to go out looking good, or as good as was possible.

Still alive at dinner time, she ate well, and stayed up late, drinking and dancing, having the time of her life, while waiting for the inevitable.

The next morning, she was surprised to wake up in her hotel bed. Turning on the news, she saw the story of an Agatha Burke, the same age as her, who had died in a freak accident the night before. Shocked, Agatha noticed the victim's name was spelled the same as the headstone shown in the crystal ball.

Confused, Agatha sought out Madame Karalita.

The fortune teller said her old crystal ball had been defective, but she had warned Agatha about finding out such information. She also suggested Agatha hadn't been clear about the spelling of her name.

Agatha demanded to know her true date of death, and this time she was very clear about how to spell her name.

And so, dear Reader, we leave Agatha, broke, with no home and with bills coming due, and knowing she's got another twenty-five years to live.

Grimoire

Settle in dear Reader, while I tell you the strange tale of Kylie, who loved power over others, but finally met someone who wouldn't tolerate her behaviour.

Kylie always knew she was special. Her mother, Marla Moreton, was a high powered barrister, who never lost a case, and who always told Kylie to never back down.

Kylie took it to heart. All through school, she bullied other children. She did all the standard things, taking weaker kids' lunch money, giving horrible nicknames to kids, that all the other kids mimicked, rather than earn her wrath. Kids not as smart as her were labelled "stupid". Kids smarter than her were "ugly." She openly defied teachers.

Any time an attempt was made to discipline Kylie, Marla would appear, threatening lawsuits the school could not afford.

So right through primary school, Kylie always got her own way at school.

At home, there was a long string of child carers and housekeepers who quit because of Kylie's behaviour. Marla would never hear a bad word said about her. She constantly told Kylie to always stand her ground and remember her strength, that she was a from a long line of strong, powerful, women.

Kylie began high school with the same kind of power over other kids as she'd always had. Her grip on teachers loosened a little, as there were far more of them, and they were more used to students trying to intimidate them.

Then in grade ten something strange happened. Cassandra started at her school. Cassandra just refused to be bullied. When Kylie called her names, she laughed. When Kylie shoved her, Cassandra didn't react at all. Where other kids lost their balance and stumbled, Cassandra just stood solid. Nothing Kylie could do seemed to intimidate Cassandra at all.

Eventually Kylie complained to her mother.

Marla opened a door concealed by a bookcase in her office. It lead to a small store room, filled with books, candles, strange jars and bottles and weird items Kylie couldn't identify.

"I always thought this was a panic room," Kylie said.

"Moreton women don't panic," Marla said. "And we don't let others deny our power either."

Marla picked up a very old book, and handed it to Kylie. She said, "This is our family grimoire. Every generation has put their own spells in it, as I have added mine, and you will add your own eventually. It will tell you all you need to know to defeat your enemy."

"Witches?" Kylie asked. "We're witches? Why didn't you tell me?"

"I've spent your entire life telling you to embrace your power, what did you think I meant?"

"Just to be strong, not... this."

"Study the book. Learn who you are."

Kylie did study, just as well as she ever studied at school.

She started with what seemed simple spells. She made a straw broom into a flying broomstick, then realised how useless that was, when everyone would see her flying it. She flicked through the book, noticing that some were marked with notes from women in her family, which said things like, "be careful", "don't do lightly".

Amid the spells and potions, were long essays by women she didn't know, or didn't remember, which were just not worth the effort to read. One was about "blood magic" which said something about blood magic being particularly powerful.

She didn't read further, but went looking for blood spells to find something that would defeat the hated Cassandra.

At last she found a spell "Potion for a witch to defeat the will of an enemy."

Now, dear Reader, I'm sure you paid attention in English class and know who is the subject and who is the object in the name of that spell. What a pity Kylie hadn't paid such close attention!

The first ingredient on the list was: "The subject's blood."

In physical education class, Kylie made sure to hit Cassandra in the face with a netball. She threw the ball hard enough to cause a bleeding nose. At the end of the lesson, Kylie surreptitiously removed the bloody tissues from the rubbish bin.

She carefully followed the recipe, and made the potion, using blood-soaked tissues when blood was called for. She breathed deeply of the purple mist that erupted from the cauldron.

The next day at school, Kylie cornered Cassandra and said, "Give me your lunch money or else."

Cassandra calmly answered, "No. Please go away."

Kylie immediately turned and walked away, not knowing why she did so.

Later, Kylie was calling a girl names, and Cassandra, who was nearby, said, "Oh leave her alone."

Kylie again just stopped what she was doing, and walked away. She still didn't know why.

At the end of the school day, Kylie was demanding another girl do her homework for her. Cassandra was walking past, and said, "Just do your own homework. You're not the queen."

Kylie rushed home and started doing her homework, a thing she hadn't done in years.

She was finishing when Marla came home, flustered.

"What's wrong?" Kylie asked. She'd never seen her mother anything but calm.

"The queen is coming to dinner," Marla said.

"Queen?"

"The Witch Queen! I didn't even know she was in town, but she moved here a couple of months ago. She wants to see us. Her daughter, the Princess Cassandra told her you were abusing your power at school. So tell me again about this girl who was causing you problems, and what you've done about her."

So, dear Reader, we leave Kylie and Marla, about to face the most awkward dinner of their lives.

Tree

Settle in, dear Reader, while I tell you the strange tale of Anna, who learned the hard way not to pick on little kids.

Anna had to stay at her little cousin Kayla's house for a week while her mother was in hospital. Worse, she had to share Kayla's room.

Anna had argued with her mother, had pointed out that no fifteen year old wanted to share a room with a five year old, had insisted she was old enough to stay home alone.

Despite that, her Aunt Mary and Uncle Jake had taken her home with them, after dropping her mother at the hospital.

Anna sulked that afternoon. She spent most of the afternoon on her computer, or playing with her phone. As much as possible, she tried to ignore her cousin.

Eventually Aunt Mary strongly suggested she go outside and play with Kayla for a while, since Kayla had been looking forward to spending time with her.

Resentfully, Anna went out to the back yard, where Kayla was playing with a doll.

"Anna, this is Chrissy. She's my favourite doll. We have tea parties together. Do you want a tea party?"

"No. I'm not a baby, and I don't play tea parties." Anna went to go and sit under a tree to text a friend, and try to continue to ignore Kayla.

"Not that tree!" Kayla shrieked. "That's the monster tree. Stay away from the monster tree."

"Monster tree? Seriously? OK. What makes you think it's a monster tree?"

"At night time, if you look at it out the window, it has a scary face, and it moves, and if you don't hide it will get you."

81

"Look," Anna said. "The tree's got rough bark. Maybe at night, the shadows make it look like it's got a scary face. Maybe you just imagine it. Babies imagine things all the time."

"I'm not a baby! I'm a big girl. I go to school."

"Prep's not real school. It's not real school until you're in grade one, and even then that's only primary school. Prep's just baby school."

"You're a big meanie. I hope the monster tree gets you."

Kayla walked away with her doll to play in another part of the yard.

Anna, feeling victorious, sat back under the monster tree, and texted her best friend Kerry all about the conversation.

When Aunt Mary called them in for dinner, Kerry texted to be careful the monster tree didn't get her. The text made Anna laugh.

How often, dear Reader, are the things small children say discounted or ignored?

That night, after Anna had complained again about having to sleep on a trundle bed in Kayla's room, she stood beside the window, looking out over the back yard. Kayla had gone to bed hours earlier, and Anna could hear her deep, regular breathing.

In the moonlight, Anna could clearly see the scary face on the monster tree. No wonder Kayla had been scared. That face, with the jagged toothy mouth, was guaranteed to frighten any small child.

Anna took a photo. She texted it to Kerry, with a message saying, "I guess there was a reason Kayla thought the tree was a monster."

She looked up from texting. Strange. The tree looked closer. Anna thought the light must have shifted.

82

A text came back from Kerry: "Watch out it doesn't get you."

Anna looked down at her phone to read the text, then looked back up.

The tree seemed closer, still. Of course, that was impossible. Anna looked at her photo. The tree had been back behind the clothesline. It was parallel to it now. That couldn't be right. She re-checked the photo.

Then she looked out the window yet again, to see the tree was almost against the glass.

At that moment Kayla woke up, and squealed: "Hide!"

Kayla pulled the covers up over her head. Anna dived under Kayla's bed, dropping her phone, and shattering the glass.

"How long do we have to keep hiding?" Anna whispered.

"Until morning," Kayla whispered back.

The next day, Kayla was up early, and out playing, before Anna woke up.

Anna was sore and stiff from sleeping on the floor under Kayla's bed. She didn't see Kayla run over to the monster tree and throw her arms around it in a hug, or hear her thanking the tree for helping teach Anna to not be so mean.

And so, dear Reader, we leave Anna, who has learned her lesson about taking her resentment out on smaller and weaker people. She's going to be much nicer to her little cousin for the rest of her stay.

The Best

I invite you, dear Reader, to get comfortable. Settle in as I tell you the strange tale of Samantha, who just wanted to excel at something, anything. Well, really, she just wanted her parents to notice her.

Sam was an ordinary teenager. She did slightly above average in school. She did slightly below average in sports. She did average in music and art. As it averages out, she was entirely average.

This would have been fine, except Sam had a sister two years older, named Madison. Maddy excelled at everything.

Again, that would have been fine, if not for the way their parents treated their difference.

Every day, Sam would hear how great Maddy was. Maddy made their parents proud winning the art contest Sam came fifth in. The whole family had to go see Maddy play piano at their music school's half-yearly recital. Sam loved her guitar, but didn't play quite well enough to be selected to perform.

The family always went out to dinner to celebrate Maddy's great test results. Maddy always scored ninety-eight or ninety-nine percent and always received an A plus, of course.

Sam's favourite school subject was English. She loved creative writing. Even her teacher, however, told her that while her writing was good, it was nowhere near as good as her sister's.

Sam was an ordinary kid, who was lost against the extraordinariness of her sister.

At Christmas time the whole extended family got together, at Sam's Aunt Olivia's house. Olivia was CEO for a multi-national company. She had a huge house which could easily fit everyone.

Sam's parents proudly boasted to her father's parents and siblings about all of Maddy's achievements for the year.

Aunt Olivia listened to her brother and sister-in-law boasting about their golden child, and asked, "And how was Sam's year, Charlie?"

Sam's father seemed startled at his sister's question. "Well," he said. "Sam just keeps on keeping on. She's a trier, which is fine."

"What are her interests?"

"Her interests? Well, she's a teenager, she likes clothes and makeup and things."

Aunt Olivia continued, "She's not wearing make-up. Maybe she doesn't like make-up and things. You don't actually notice her. Like Mum and Dad didn't notice me and you got all the attention, right up until uni? Because for some reason, being the best is the only thing that matters in this family. You didn't learn anything at all, did you? You didn't learn how much resentment builds up when one kid is the favourite and the other's just extra."

Sam's father seemed surprised, "What was there to learn? I just put in more effort than you. Then in uni, you finally applied yourself."

"No. I didn't finally apply myself. I was always smart. I always put in the effort. It's just that because you were a superstar, our parents couldn't be bothered noticing me. I spent all of my childhood and most of my teens totally ignored by our parents. Now you and Cherise are doing the same to Sam. Wake up to yourselves. You're terrible parents, just like our parents were."

At this point, Sam's grandparents entered the argument, claiming they'd always treated both children fairly. They insisted Olivia would not have been so successful without the incentive of needing to prove herself.

So dear Reader, we'll leave the family to get over that little squabble. No-one's leaving in a huff, not when they can enjoy Olivia's lovely house and the expensive food she's supplied. Let's come back to them a bit later, after the eating and the gifts.

Olivia took Sam aside. "I have an extra present for you," she said. She gave Sam a gold trophy with the number one engraved on it.

"It's a trophy. What's it for?" Sam was clearly confused.

"It's for everything. It was given to me when I was a little older than you are now. It changed my life. Just keep it somewhere safe. As long as it's in your possession, it will make a difference."

Sam thought the trophy was a weird gift. It didn't have a name on it, or what event it was awarded for, or anything else to indicate its past. It was old, Sam could tell, since it was worn and scratched. Strange as it was, she appreciated it, just as she appreciated her aunt for standing up for her.

At home, Sam put the old trophy in the back of her wardrobe, and forgot about it.

School resumed, and something strange happened. Sam began getting a hundred percent on all her assignments.

She decided she wouldn't tell her parents her results until they asked about them, which would probably be when they received the school reports at the end of semester.

She wrote a story for English which was so good her teacher wanted to submit it to a magazine to be published. Sam took the consent form, not to her parents, but to her Aunt. Olivia was listed as an alternate contact on her school enrolment, so the signature was accepted.

Her guitar playing improved dramatically, to the point where her teacher thought she was more than ready to perform publicly.

Meanwhile, Maddy continued to do everything at her normal, excellent, level, and to gain adoration and adulation from their parents.

Sam's parents didn't notice she'd paid particular attention to her clothes and hair, and even put on make-up for the music school's next recital. The whole family was going of course, because Maddy was a star. Indeed, Maddy had performed a particularly challenging piece in the first half of the program. Maddy was not in the second half, so sat back with their family. No-one noticed Sam hadn't come back after excusing herself during intermission. Fortunately for Sam's planned surprise, the first and second halves of the program had been rehearsed separately.

When Sam's classical guitar solo was introduced, the family went scrambling through their programs, to discover that, no, it had not been a mistake. Sam's performance, of an intricate piece, was flawless, and she received a standing ovation.

In the foyer, later, Sam's stunned parents heard from all the other music school parents about how great a musician Sam was. Some of them also remembered to praise Maddy.

In the car on the way home, Sam's father asked why she hadn't told them she was in the recital this year. Sam replied that they hadn't seemed interested in how she was doing.

The year went on. Sam's parents showed more interest in her music, but in nothing else. She didn't tell them she was getting a hundred percent on all her tests. She watched as they gushed over Maddy's ninety-eights and ninety-nines, and said nothing.

When she received a copy of a literary magazine with her story in it, Sam said nothing. Maddy, however, found it on Sam's desk, while she was looking for a pencil to borrow.

Maddy took the magazine to show their parents.

The family went out to dinner, to Maddy's favourite restaurant, to celebrate Sam being published. Her father asked how much help Maddy had given her with the story. Both Sam and Maddy denied any collaboration on Sam's work.

It was also Maddy who first found out that Sam was doing so well in school. She asked Sam why she would keep it quiet.

Sam said Aunt Olivia had been right, being the kid who got no attention was awful, and she didn't want to be part of making Maddy feel as bad as she had done for so many years.

Maddy had not realised that by keeping quiet and just accepting how things were, she had been part of hurting Sam so much. She apologised, and the two made a pact that from then on, they would not be part of making either of them feel less important.

When end of semester exams came around, their parents again made a fuss over Maddy and offered to go to her favourite restaurant. Maddy suggested Sam might have a turn to choose.

Their father said, no. It was Maddy's reward for working so hard. Maddy said Sam had worked hard too, and suggested they look at her exam results.

So, a week before report cards were due out, their parents finally asked to see Sam's exam results. She'd kept the whole semester's worth of exams and assignments together in a folder, and so was easily able to present them all.

The parents went through her semester's work, seeing the hundred percent over and over and over, and all the glowing praise from teachers.

"Why didn't you tell us about your results," her mother asked.

"You never asked," Sam said with a shrug. "I thought you weren't interested."

"That's not true, we were always interested," her mother said.

"Yet you never asked," Sam replied. "So I kept it all together in case you eventually did ask."

"Can Sam choose the restaurant now?" Maddy asked.

"Did you help Sam with her work?" their father asked.

"No," Maddy said. "I did not help her with all her work for the whole semester. I was way too focussed on my own. I'm always afraid that if I don't do well, you'll lose interest in me too, which you're probably going to do now that you know Sam's smarter than me."

"We wouldn't do that," their mother seemed shocked at the thought.

"You've done it to Sam for our whole lives," Maddy countered. "I found out she was getting good results at school before you did. I learned about her published story before you did. Well now we're each the top of our class for everything, but her grades are slightly higher than mine. Are you going to notice her now? Will you still notice me?"

"We're not accepting you playing favourites any more," Sam said. "We both matter. We know that. We deserve parents who know that."

So dear Reader, we leave Sam and Maddy's parents to deal with a reality where both of their children matter. When this generation grows up, they're not going to play favourites with their own children.

Meeting Death

I invite you, dear Reader, to get comfortable. Settle in while I tell you the strange tale of Noela, who made a deal with death and lived, or rather, didn't live, to regret it.

Noela was an ordinary woman. She wasn't especially pretty, or especially successful, or especially popular, or especially smart, or especially talented. She was just another very ordinary person in a world of very ordinary people.

She worked a very ordinary data entry job. She'd gone to a very ordinary school. She'd come from a very ordinary family, well, with one exception.

Some people, dear Reader, can be happy living very ordinary lives. Noela was not one of those people. She raged against her ordinariness. She raged against people who were not as ordinary as her. One of those, specifically, was her sister.

Noela's sister Jody, was not ordinary. She was extraordinarily beautiful. She was extraordinarily talented. She was extraordinarily successful. She was extraordinarily smart.

Their parents had not treated them differently growing up, but everyone around them had. Next to the radiant Jody, Noela had always slipped into the background.

While mousy Noela worked data-entry, glamorous Jody was a successful movie star.

While boring Noela went home alone to her empty flat each night, Jody partied and came home to a wealthy, handsome husband, and beautiful twin children.

While Noela struggled to pay her bills, Jody hired staff to cook, clean, care for her children, manage her diary and deal with the bills.

While Noela was never noticed, Jody was always in the spotlight.

"Resentment" was too weak a word for what Noela felt towards her sister.

Noela was drinking coffee at her desk. Her computer was misbehaving. She had a call in to IT, but they were slow coming.

She was taking a sip of her coffee when she heard a sudden buzzing noise from the computer. It startled her, making her drop her coffee. Coffee spread over the keyboard. Noela grabbed the cup. The wet, malfunctioning electrics shocked her.

There was a sudden pain, and then Noela felt nothing, a total absence of any sensation. She could not feel herself breathing or her heart beating. She could not hear any sound. Her peripheral vision lost focus. All she could see was straight in front of her.

There, she could see a skeletal figure in a hooded robe, holding a scythe.

Was this someone's idea of a joke?

Why was someone dressed as the Grim Reaper in her office?

She tried to ask what was going on, but had no voice.

The figure pointed ahead, indicating for her to go that way.

She tried again.

She felt, rather than heard, a reply. The reply was she was dead, and must go where the Reaper pointed.

No, she tried to say. She didn't want to go anywhere.

Again she felt the reply, she must. A person had died, a soul must go where the Reaper tells them to.

No. She was definite. She would not.

The reply she felt was that it would be a mistake to refuse.

Could the Reaper take another soul instead, if a soul absolutely had to go? She suggested the Reaper take Jody's soul. Jody had already enjoyed everything life had to give, and Noela had not.

She felt the reply, if Noela did not go where directed, she would have to stay with her body. Also, Noela would be responsible if her sister's soul was taken in her place.

Noela agreed she would be responsible, whatever that cost was.

Noela stayed, her vision cleared. She could clearly see her body slumped over her computer. She saw her co-workers gathering around. She watched her body taken first to a morgue, and autopsied. She was sure she should have felt sick, watching, but all she felt was a detached interest.

Then her body went to the funeral parlour. She saw Jody, crying over her body, insisting on being the one to do her hair and make-up, not allowing the professionals to do it.

Noela thought Jody was making it all about herself, that the grief was an act. Or perhaps, without her soul, Jody simply couldn't hold it all together.

Tied to her body, Noela couldn't follow Jody.

Noela accompanied her body to the church on the day of the funeral.

There was Jody, her make-up streaked with tears. She didn't look so beautiful any more. Jody was leaning on the handsome husband, the beautiful twins, hanging on to them, sobbing.

Noela wondered if it perhaps wasn't an act after all. She wondered if it wasn't having her soul taken either. Perhaps it was genuine grief.

Jody gave a eulogy. She talked about Noela being the person who supported her and believed in her the most, how she'd believed she would never have achieved anything without Noela. She talked about their childhood together, how Noela had always been the one who looked out for her.

Jody broke down sobbing, and finished her eulogy with her nose running, mascara in rivulets down her face.

The funeral moved to the cemetery. Noela realised her error. If she could only go where her body went, would she be stuck underground now, for ever? And what about Jody? Had the Reaper actually taken her soul at Noela's request? What did that mean?

Noela saw her coffin being lowered. She followed it, unable to do otherwise.

As dirt started falling in on her, she saw the skeletal figure of the Reaper again, once again pointing a direction for her to go.

She started to follow, stopped, and tried to say she was sorry for the deal she tried to make. Was there any way to give Jody's soul back to her.

She felt the answer. There had never been any deal. No-one could bargain with death.

So, dear Reader, we leave Noela, moving on, and her bereft sister, Jody learning to live without her.

What If?

I invite you dear Reader to get comfortable, settle in while I tell you the strange tale of Janelle, who wanted to change some of the choices she'd made.

We all have crossroads in our lives, times when we must choose one thing or another. Many of us have "what if" moments, wondering how our lives would have turned out if we'd chosen differently.

Crossroads aren't only places to make choices. They used to be where executed criminals were buried, so their ghosts wouldn't know the way back to their judges, juries, or executioners were. Crossroads were also where people made deals with demons.

Janelle was not happy with her life.

When she was only twenty she'd been engaged. But the man she'd been engaged to often said cruel and belittling things to her, compared her unfavourably to other women, took her for granted. In one of those of crossroads of life, Janelle made a decision. To the surprise of her fiancé, and the horror of her parents, she broke off the engagement.

Some years alter, at another point of crossroads, she had married another man. This man said all of the right things. It was only once they were married and had children, that his true nature showed itself. He said the right things in public. In private, he did all of the wrong things.

He wasted all of his own money and most of hers, leaving her little to support them and their children with. He berated her if she dared to express her own thoughts or feelings, and encouraged the children to disrespect her. Whenever she said "no" to the children, he said "yes," so the children learned that she had no authority.

Eventually, things were so bad, she found herself at another crossroads moment. She got a divorce. She found herself a single mother, supporting two children who had no respect for her, with no help whatsoever from their father, but at least she was allowed her own thoughts and feelings.

Over years, she struggled, and built a different relationship with her children. She was tired. Trying to establish a home and financial life, with no resources and two children took everything out of her. She started to wonder where she'd made the mistake. Was it breaking off that first engagement? Was it in getting married to her ex-husband? What if she could go back, would she do something differently?

So dear Reader, Janelle did a thing only a desperate person would do. She went to a physical crossroads in a quiet country area and attempted to summon a demon. She guessed there was probably meant to be a ritual or a sacrifice, or something, but she didn't know what or how. So she stood at a quiet crossroads and said, "Is anyone there? I think I want to make a deal."

She stood there, looking around. Of course there was no-one there. Feeling foolish, she started to walk back to where she'd parked her car.

Almost at the car, she turned and looked back over her shoulder, to see a man, dressed in a business suit, standing there. There was something compelling about him.

He said, "You want to make a deal?"

"Ah, yes, um," Janelle was suddenly unsure of the wisdom of her quest. "I want to know what my life would have been like, if I had made other choices."

"I can send you back to where you can make those other choices. I will let you remember the life you've had. You can compare. When you get to today's date, come back here and tell me which life you wish to live from that point."

"O... K...., and ah," she was uncertain how to phrase the question.

"The price?"

"Yeah, that."

"Oh, you know the price. Do we have a deal?"

"Yes."

Janelle was twenty again.

This time, she decided to live with the put-downs, knowing how much worse things could be.

After marriage and children, the put-downs only got worse.

After years of being told how useless and worthless she was, she believed it. Her children believed it.

When she found out her husband had been cheating on her she simply accepted it as the natural result of her not being attractive or smart or worthy. She remembered in the other timeline she'd found the courage and strength for a divorce, but that must have just been a dream, because she knew she wasn't smart of strong enough to do anything like that.

Janelle was ground down further than she would previously have believed any person could be, when one day she found herself at that same crossroads.

"Well?" The man asked.

Janelle suddenly realised she had gone back to the wrong crossroads. She should have gone back to the one where she was married, when she could have said "no", and gone on to live alone, or perhaps eventually found a truly loving partner.

She said this to the man.

He smiled broadly. "No," he said. "Our agreement was that you would either choose to continue to live this timeline, or go back to the one you were originally on."

"Can we renegotiate?"

"For what? There's nothing else you can pay."

Janelle chose her original life, because in that the pain of divorce and starting over again had already happened, and she had already begun to live an independent, if difficult, life.

So, dear Reader, we leave Janelle, knowing her life could have been worse. She has no idea that an angel, who sometimes impersonates a demon, proud of her strength, and sometimes tweaks small things in her favour. Oh, and that timeline he wouldn't let her try? In that she would have been hit by a truck and killed, at the time she was otherwise getting married.

Ghost

I invite you dear Reader to get comfortable, settle in while I tell you the strange tale of Amy, who definitely did not believe in the supernatural.

It was the thirty-first of October when Amy moved into her new house. Or rather it was a very old house, but new to her.

She was surprised to see houses around had Halloween decorations out. She'd thought that nonsense had died out over COVID.

Amy sighed. After mass produced junk food, this nonsense was the latest unnecessary import from America.

It was unhealthy, she thought, this horror-for-fun thing that began in horror movies. Death and violence were not or entertaining, she thought.

After the removalists left, Amy decided unpacking boxes could wait until morning. She sat on the front verandah, and used her mobile phone to order pizza.

A woman, who appeared to be in her early twenties, approached her. "Hi, I'm Kate. I live next door."

Amy introduced herself.

"I guess you noticed Halloween's kind of a thing in this area. We buy lots of extra lollies. I'm happy to give you some to hand out, if you want to join in."

"I don't think I'll join in," Amy said. "I'm not really into the whole ghosts and goblins thing."

"But you bought the haunted house! I thought you'd be really into the paranormal thing."

"Haunted house," Amy snorted, despite her attempt to be polite. "I don't believe in that kind of thing."

"Oh it's true. The first owner was some kind of spiritualist, or Satanist, or something. The story changes with whoever's telling it."

"Stories usually do."

"Then there were a whole string of people who owned it, they either moved out straight after moving in or they died here."

"I understood the previous owner lived here for forty years."

"Elsie, yes. She and her husband bought the house when they were newlyweds, she told me. Her husband died a couple of years later, hanged himself on the verandah here. Elsie said she only stayed because her husband was one of the ghosts."

"That's some story. So what happened to Elsie? Did she move to a nursing home?"

"No, she was only sixty-two. No. She cut her wrists in the bathroom."

"Well, that's charming."

"Anyway, when you see them, what Elsie said was that they were all just death echoes. They were trapped reliving their deaths, kind of like memories. She said there was nothing really malevolent in the house, you just had to be willing to live with seeing people die over and over. Although, I guess, in the end she couldn't live with that any more."

Amy's pizza arrived. She excused herself to go inside and eat her dinner. Kate went back to her own yard, as small fairies, monsters, movie characters and other beings began to knock on doors.

So dear Reader, Amy had heard the story of her new home, and didn't believe any of it. She turned off the outside lights and tried to do anything in her power to not appear to be home. She didn't answer the frequent knocks on the door.

99

Amy was putting leftover pizza in the fridge, when we saw something white moving in the hallway. She went to investigate, and saw what seemed to be a person dressed in a sheet. That had to be the worst costume anyone had ever come up with, she thought.

"Hey!" She called out, "get out of my house. This is private property."

The sheeted figure moved silently past her, and she felt cold air travel past with it. The figure went to the stove and turned it on, lighting the gas jet. That was impossible. It was a modern electric stove, but here the figure was lighting the gas, and catching the sheet on fire. The figure seemed to struggle, trying to pull the sheet off, but the flames spread rapidly, and the figure lay on the floor, on fire, then suddenly disappeared.

It was certainly an elaborate practical joke, but Amy wasn't falling for it. She searched for some kind of projector, or anything that could have made someone seem to just disappear in front of her.

Perhaps they were outside. She went out to the verandah, and found a man's body hanging from the rafters. Who had put a dummy up there? She hadn't agreed to be part of this stupid Halloween thing. Amy dragged over a chair and climbed up, to undo the rope, but her hand went straight through the rope, before the dummy and rope disappeared.

"This isn't funny. Stop it!" She called out, thinking the prankster must hear her.

Obviously Kate was in on it, since she was the one who had come with the story to set the whole prank up, but who else? Why would her new neighbours who didn't even know her want to play such stupid tricks on her?

"If this continues, I'm calling the police," she said, again just trusting the pranksters heard.

After a stressful day, perhaps she could just relax with a bath. Hopefully whoever was pulling the prank would back off now they knew she intended to report them.

She turned on the light in the bathroom, to see a middle aged woman sitting in a tub of bloody water.

"This isn't funny. And this is really taking it too far," Amy said as she reached to grab the woman's arm. Her hand went straight through. The woman simply disappeared.

That was the limit for Amy, she called the police.

A police car with two officers came. She told them what had been happening, and explained that the only person in the neighbourhood she had met was Kate from next door, and that Kate had set up this whole horrible practical joke.

Police searched the house, and found no sign of any intruders.

They went next door to talk to Kate.

Then they came back, and explained that no-one named Kate currently lived next door. The oldest daughter of the next-door family had been named Kate, but she had died the previous year. She'd been sitting on the verandah of Amy's house, talking with the previous owner, when she'd suffered a heart attack. Kate's parents had been horrified that Amy had been so cruel as to pretend their beloved daughter was involved in some crime.

So, dear Reader, we leave Amy looking for a hotel room for the night. Her house will be back on the market in the morning.

Magic Word

I invite you, dear Reader, to get comfortable, settle in while I tell you the strange tale of Maria, who thought she knew more about raising her grandchild than her daughter-in-law did.

Maria had always considered her daughter-in-law, Jade, far too permissive in how she was raising little Pippa. She was very free with her advice, but Jade appeared to not pay any attention to any of it.

In fact, Jade had gone so far as to tell Maria that all children were different, and parents had to adapt their parenting style to the needs of the child.

Maria knew that was absolute drivel, and all any child really needed was strict expectations and a firm hand.

When Jade went to hospital for an emergency appendectomy, Maria had the opportunity to prove her point. She offered to have Pippa stay with her until Jade was able to leave hospital. Her son, Bill, had gratefully accepted the offer.

Maria thought that in a couple of days, she would turn Pippa into the most polite, well-behaved version of herself that was possible. It wasn't that Pippa was a particularly naughty or ill-mannered child, just that Maria felt that she could do better.

Well, dear Reader, I'm sure you've heard that pride goes before a fall, and Maria was certainly proud enough to believe she was a far better parent than Jade could possibly be.

When Pippa put down her doll, toddled to Maria and said, "Want stwawbelly," Maria saw her chance to enforce some manners.

She said, "What's the magic word?"

Anyone who grew up with parents asking for the magic word would know that she meant "please."

Pippa, however, knew another magic word. She said, "Abacabara," which was a fairly good attempt at "abracadabra" for her age.

Instantly, a strawberry appeared in Pippa's hand. She toddled off happily, eating her prize.

Maria stared, open-mouthed, at the child.

Then, in a panic, she rang Bill, who was waiting for Jade to come out of surgery. Frantically, Maria told him what had happened.

Bill said matter-of-factly, "If you wanted her to say 'please', you should have told her to say 'please'. If you tell her you want a magic word, she's going to give you a magic word. Kids are very literal at that age."

Maria insisted that Bill was missing the point; that the magic word had caused magic to happen.

He, with strained patience, replied, "That's what magic words are meant to do." He said he had to go because Jade was being moved back to the ward.

Maria looked suspiciously at Pippa, who was back playing quietly with her doll.

Then she had a thought and asked, "Can you get other things with your magic word?"

Pippa stopped making the doll dance, looked up at her grandmother, and said, "Yes."

"Let's play a game," Maria said. "I'll say a thing, and you use your magic to get it. Doesn't that sound like fun?"

Pippa looked at her doubtfully. "Mummy says no," she said.

"Mummy's not here," Maria said, conspiratorially. "Let's just try one thing. Can you use your word to get money."

103

Pippa thought a moment, and said, "Abacabara." Instantly, there was a pile of play money on the floor next to where Pippa was playing.

"Can you get real money? You know, like Mummy and Daddy use at the shops?"

Pippa tried again, and a plastic card appeared on the pile. Two-year-olds , it must be said, are not known for their literacy and numeracy. Because Pippa had no idea what the marks on the card were supposed to be, they were just strange scribbles.

Maria tried something else. "Do you remember Grandpa? Can you get Grandpa?"

Pippa used her word again.

The smell arrived first, then the rotting body of Maria's three-months-dead husband opened the front door, and walked in. Maria gagged and screamed alternately. Her husband's rotting corpse sat in an arm chair. Finally, she found some words and yelled, "Send him back! Send him back!"

Pippa used her word, and the body was gone, but the smell lingered.

Maria ran around the house opening windows. Then she found room deodoriser spray, and sprayed it everywhere.

Pippa watched her grandmother scrambling around, with great interest. Then she said, "Draw now?"

"Yes, I'll get you something to draw with," Maria said quickly. She scrambled to find paper and pens.

Pippa sat her doll down beside her, and began drawing.

Maria sat on the lounge chair beside where the child was drawing. "Let's not use the magic word any more," she said.

"Mummy says no," Pippa said, knowingly.

"Mummy's right," Maria found herself forced to agree.

So, dear Reader, we leave Maria, who has discovered that not all children are the same, and that parents might actually know their own child's needs.

Dress

Settle in dear Reader, while I tell you the strange tale of Jasmine, who just wanted to do normal teenage stuff, but her father was unwilling to allow it.

Jasmine's mother had died when she was quite young.

As Jasmine grew, her father had provided for all her needs, but not anything extra, or fun.

When she wanted to learn ballet, or art, or sport, he told her those were unnecessary frivolities, and not worth the money or time they would take.

He told her the only things worth learning were things that would lead to a career.

She had begun taking over cooking meals during her primary school years. When other girls were visiting each other's homes, to play with dolls, she was planning meals and making grocery lists. When other girls attended after school activities, she was cooking.

By the time she reached high school, she had taken on most of the house work. Her world was school and home, until she turned sixteen and persuaded her father that a part time job would be a good preparation for a future career. Her father, however, would not let her keep her earnings, insisting that she was too young to understand how to manage money.

Her wardrobe consisted of her school and work uniforms, and three sets of jeans and shirts, as her father did not believe she needed anything more.

Now, she was seventeen. The end of year twelve was approaching. She had filled in her forms for university, deliberately putting unis in other cities ahead of local ones. She knew her marks were good enough to get her in anywhere, and hoped her father would allow her to have the money he was saving for her so she could go. She didn't care where she would go, she just wanted to leave.

She'd never been to a school dance, but begged her father to allow her to go to her formal, her last chance at a school dance.

He did not see the point.

Jasmine did something she reserved for the direst of needs: she called her aunt, her father's older sister. Aunt Jane had stood up for her when she first began her periods, explaining to Jasmine's father, that yes, Jasmine did absolutely need products to manage it, and that it wasn't a choice.

After Jasmine's call, Jane appeared at the door, in a flurry of outrage. Jasmine could almost convince herself she could see steam coming from her aunt's ears.

A woman on a definite mission, Jane marched into Jasmine's father's office.

Jasmine could hear her aunt yell: "Gary, you have got to be kidding! Do you remember your formal? Remember how excited you were to go with Ellie? You don't think Jas deserves that same excitement?"

"She doesn't have a date. She can't go to a formal alone."

"And how was she supposed to get a date? You've never allowed her a life. When you're old and wondering why she never calls, this will be why."

"I don't know what to do with her. Ellie's not around to tell me what to do with her."

"That's been your excuse for sixteen of the seventeen years Jas has been alive. It's past time you got over yourself and acted like a father, instead of a prison warden. Now, what have you got to say for yourself?"

"She looks like Ellie."

"She looks a bit like Ellie."

"If I let her go out, and something happened to her, it would be like losing Ellie all over again."

"No. It would be losing Jasmine. If you don't let her have a life, she will leave as soon as she's eighteen, and you will lose her anyway. Is that what you want? She's not a substitute for Ellie. She's her own person, and she's practically an adult."

"OK, she can go."

"Good. Now, I understand you have all her money. You need to let her have money for a dress and make-up and shoes."

"What? No! She's going to need her money for her education. She can't just go and waste it on something so frivolous."

"She can't go in school uniform."

"She can wear one of Ellie's old dresses."

"You're kidding? Sixteen years and you've still got Ellie's clothes? Right, well, if that's all she's allowed, you're going to let her choose what she wants, and make adjustments. And she get's to use Ellie's jewellery, too, right?"

Jane came out of the office, looked at Jasmine and said, "You heard all that?"

Jasmine was in tears. "I have to wear one of my mother's old dresses?"

"Don't worry, kid. We've got this."

Jane led Jasmine to Gary's bedroom and opened the walk-in wardrobe. More than half of the wardrobe held beautiful, glamorous, dresses, all covered in plastic from the dry cleaner's.

"We're going to have to choose a dress and get it cleaned after sitting so long. Lucky for you, your mother had excellent taste. What do you like?"

Jasmine had never seen her mother's dresses before. They were glorious rich colours, in satins and silks.

She chose a beautiful red satin dress.

With her aunt's help, she made adjustments for size. Then Jane suggested dressing the dress up a bit more, for the formality of the event. She went to Ellie's jewellery boxes, and found several strings of pearls.

"These are relatively inexpensive. I wouldn't dare do this with her really good stuff," Jane explained, as she cut the strings. "Now let's plan out a design, and I'll teach you some beading skills."

They highlighted the dress with swirling designs in white pearls, and found a black belt to go with the outfit.

Jasmine hesitantly tried on her mother's shoes, and found she was the same size. She chose a pair of high heels, and practised walking in them.

On the night of the formal, Jane came to their house, bringing make-up. She did Jasmine's make-up and styled her hair.

Once she was ready, Jane insisted Jasmine show her father what she looked like. Gary seemed close to crying.

Jane drove Jasmine to the formal and promised to come back for her at the end of the evening.

So, dear Reader, it seemed Jasmine had found a fairy godmother in her aunt, but the evening's real magic wasn't for her. It was for her father.

Gary sat on the couch, his head in his hands. For the first time, he'd realised his daughter really was growing up. What if she really did plan to leave him?

He felt the slight movement of someone sitting beside him on the couch. Ellie's voice said, "Our daughter's grown into a beautiful young woman."

Gary looked up. There was Ellie, wearing the same red dress Jasmine had just gone out in, but without the pearl beading.

"Did I do it right?" He asked. "I didn't know what to do without you."

"I would have done it differently, let her have a childhood," Ellie said it kindly, without judgement. "But you did what you were able to do. Perhaps now, you could loosen the reins just a little? Let her have her own money, let Jane teach her about make-up, the girly things she's missed out on? She really needs a drivers' licence. She'll need it for uni. You know that's only months away. And she needs clothes, and time with people her age."

"Why didn't you ever come to me before, tell me this?"

"I think it was the dress, that's what woke me up, her wearing it."

"Can you stay with me now? I haven't known how to go on without you?"

"I don't know if I can. But I do know, we have a daughter who needs you. She needs you to be a real father, not a taskmaster, not a financial controller. Instead of preserving all my clothes and possessions locked away, instead of keeping your love and compassion locked away, you need to live your life. And you need to encourage our daughter to live hers. This grumpy, intolerant man, who just makes rules and says 'no' all the time isn't the man I married, isn't the man I loved. You need to be that man again. Jasmine needs you to be him as well."

"I'm sorry. I know I've done it all wrong. I'll try."

"I know you will. And please, tell her I'm proud of her. When you give yourself a chance to actually see her and know her, you'll be proud of her, too."

Suddenly, inexplicably, Ellie was gone. For a moment, Gary felt he'd lost her all over again.

110

He thought for a few moments, and called Jane. He told her he would pick Jasmine up from the formal.

The next day he insisted on taking her out to buy new clothes for uni, and to look at second-hand cars. He promised he would buy her the car of her choice, within limits, when she got her licence.

So dear Reader, we leave Jasmine, who at last has the father she needed and deserved all along, and we leave Gary, a proud father, who has at last realised just how amazing his daughter really is.

Social Media

In invite you dear Reader to settle in, get comfortable, while I tell you the strange tale of Miranda, who found herself the target of online bullies.

Miranda made a simple post about a health issue she was facing. She thought a couple of her friends might notice and comment on it, perhaps giving her some support for a challenge that lay ahead.

People she didn't know noticed.

A strange woman she'd never had any contact with started attacking her, claiming she was transgender.

Miranda wasn't trans, but didn't see that even if she had been that would be a reason for strangers to attack her.

Another woman joined in, claiming that because of Miranda, women's public toilets weren't safe, that women would be vulnerable when they were naked in the toilet.

Other joined in.

Miranda was confused by the claims. She pointed out that outside of cubicles, women were fully dressed in public toilets.

They scoffed at her, told her she didn't know what she was talking about, and presented weirder and weirder scenarios where women might be naked.

Some of them told her they hoped she'd bleed out and die.

As their statements got angrier and angrier, and less and less rational, Miranda had a sudden realisation. She realised that these "women" attacking her had themselves never been inside a women's toilet. That was the only possible explanation for their increasingly bizarre scenarios they were posting as they attacked her. They were men, using a made-up argument to bully a woman they didn't know.

Now, dear Reader, Miranda had her own special way of dealing with bullies.

She pulled the cloth cover off her crystal ball. Focussing on the first person who had attacked her, ostensibly a middle-aged woman named Mary, Miranda watched the coloured clouds in the crystal ball swirl. Then the image settled.

Miranda replied to "Mary": "I see you Peter, with the chip crumbs and soft drink stains on your shirt, using aggression towards a woman you don't know to try to feel somehow better about yourself. You'll never fill that gap unless you get some self respect."

Miranda watched him through the crystal ball, as he read her post, and looked around trying to see how someone could be watching him. Miranda gave the crystal ball a sharp tap.

Peter leapt as electricity, not enough to kill, but definitely enough to startle coursed through his body.

Miranda wrote: "Uncomfortable Peter? How many women have you made uncomfortable with your trolling posts? You're on my radar now. Don't let me catch you mistreating another woman."

Moving on to the next bully, Miranda focussed on the profile of "Karen," supposedly a woman in her mid-twenties. The coloured clouds swirled again, and Miranda could see him.

She typed, "I see you Dylan, fifteen years old and wearing your insecurities like the sheen on your greasy skin. You don't like how people laugh at you when you tell them you're an alpha. You look down on women, because girls your own age won't go out with you. Yet you speak to them so horribly, you drive them away."

She watched as the teen read the post, and she tapped the crystal ball firmly. He jumped as he was hit with the electric shock.

She typed again, "You've got time, Dylan. You can grow up into a decent human being. Just stop trying to be something you're not. Try just being you, not a carbon copy of the influencers you're following. They're not role models. There's a reason they live in the swampy depths of the worst corners of the internet. They can't come out into the light. They can't survive the real world. I'll be watching you Dylan, so learn to make good choices."

Miranda went to the next person to have attacked her online. This was supposedly a woman in her twenties named "Kate."

Miranda focussed on the profile, the clouds swirled again, and Miranda was surprised to see a young woman who actually matched her photo.

Instead of a public reply, Miranda sent a private message: "I see you Kate, you're hurting, so you're hurting others. I see the bruises. I see the fear. You don't have to put up with it. You are stronger than you realise. You can escape. If you need help, message me. I'll be here for you."

Miranda watched Kate read the message, and gently stroked the crystal ball. She saw Kate receive comfort and strength, stand up straighter, and begin to look determined.

"I'll keep watching you Kate. I'll be here, to lend you more strength when you need it," Miranda messaged.

So, dear Reader, we leave Miranda, who knows precisely how to deal with bullies, so if you're going to bully people online, make sure you don't pick on a real witch.

Night Mare

I invite you, dear Reader, to settle in, get comfortable as I tell you the strange tale of Angelica, who received some strange advice from her great grandmother.

When Angelica was ten, her mother took her to the place where people with Alzheimer's were stored, out of sight, and often out of mind.

The place was frightening for a young girl, but more frightening was the ancient woman they'd gone to visit. Her great grandmother didn't seem to recognise her or her mother, or know anything about the world around her.

It was a relief for Angelica when it was time to go.

As she turned to follow her mother out the door of her great grandmother's room, the woman grabbed her arm. Angelica could not believe the strength of the hand that held her belonged to the frail body of the elderly woman.

Her great grandmother said, "Beware, little Angel, of the world between, neither in sleep nor wakefulness. There you will be trapped in a world of horrors. When the Night Mare comes for you, with her shiny black coat and her blazing fire eyes, and flames surrounding her, you must mount her and ride to battle. You must take up your sword and defeat the enemy."

The old woman at last let go of Angelica's arm.

Angelica ran to her mother, who hugged her, and ushered her out of the room.

"What was Great Grandma talking about?" Angelica wanted to know.

"Maybe nothing. Maybe she was talking about lucid dreaming. That's when you know you're dreaming, and you're able to change what happens. It's a way to deal with nightmares. Maybe she learned about lucid dreaming at some time, and just remembered it. People with Alzheimer's say all kinds of things. It might not mean anything at all," her mother said.

Angelica refused to go on further visits. Her great grandmother had frightened her. She never forget the old woman's words, or the grip on her arm.

Five years later, Angelica attended her great grandmother's funeral. While the minister talked about loss and resurrection, and older family members talked about memories, Angelica heard something else. She heard her great-grandmother's voice saying, "Beware, little Angel, of the world between, neither in sleep nor wakefulness. There you will be trapped in a world of horrors. When the Night Mare comes for you, with her shiny black coat and her blazing fire eyes, and flames surrounding her, you must mount her and ride to battle. You must take up your sword and defeat the enemy."

That night, Angelica had a strange dream.

Her dream began with her walking down the street she lived in. It all seem normal, except perhaps more brightly coloured.

A smoke haze came in from the west. A bushfire, perhaps?

The smoke thickened, and Angelica turned to go home, to get out of the chocking smoke.

She became disoriented, and couldn't see where home was.

Then it appeared beside her, a large black horse, with flaming eyes and flames all around her. It was the Night Mare her great grandmother had described.

Her cat, a black cat, with white socks, called Soxxy, walked up beside her. "You have to ride the Night Mare," Soxxy said.

"Why?" Angelica asked.

"You are the new Guardian of Dreams, you were chosen by the old Guardian who has recently died. Humanity has gone without a Guardian for three days. The evil smoke is seeping into dreams everywhere, not just yours. Humans need to dream. They need their dreams to process the events of their lives. You must fight back. You must protect humanity's ability to dream. Mount your horse, take your sword, and ride."

Angelica had no idea how to get on a horse or ride one, but once she decided to do it, she found she could. Hanging on the saddle was a belt holding a sheath that contained an ornate sword. She buckled the belt around her waist.

"Now what?"

Soxxy said, "Go to the source of the smoke, it's in the collective unconscious."

"Will you come with me?"

"I will be there if you need me."

She rode, somehow knowing she was going in the right direction, even though she could only see the small distance ahead that was lighted by the flames from the Night Mare.

The source was a pit of bubbling, ever increasing, red goo.

Angelica couldn't see Soxxy nearby, but asked anyway, "Is this goo what I'm supposed to fight?"

The cat appeared out of nowhere, "Yes, that is it."

Angelica stabbed at the goo with the sword. It shrieked, and shrunk back, pulled into itself.

She stabbed again, and it pulled back further.

She spent the night stabbing at red goo, as it pulled back further.

The next morning she woke as usual, and thought it had all been a dream.

But that night she again went from a normal dream, to the smoke coming over, and the Night Mare arriving to take her to the goo to fight again.

And so, dear Reader, this pattern continued for three years before the night Angelica came to a realisation.

She was fighting the goo when she remembered what her mother had said about lucid dreaming.

For the first time in years, she asked a question. "This is the collective unconscious, right?"

Soxxy appeared and answered, "Yes."

"So this is a shared place, not just mine?"

"Yes."

She called out: "I need everyone. Everyone come to help me. Bring your swords. Help me defeat the enemy."

People began to walk out of the smoke. They brought swords. Together they fought the red goo, until it was a tiny drop. Then together they built a solid box, and sealed the tiny drop in it. After that, they all returned to their own dreams.

Angelica mounted the Night Mare once more, and they rode for the love of riding.

So, dear Reader, we leave Angelica. The Night Mare still visits her. There is no more smoke and no more red goo, but they will be ready should the evil ever return. Soxxy, who has long since died in reality, is still a faithful companion, who visits with advice for her real life, as well as for her life in the world of dreams.

Curse

Settle in dear Reader, while I tell you the strange tale of Karen, who never felt she had the respect she deserved, but who finally got exactly what she deserved.

Karen was a middle aged woman who had a sense of entitlement almost too large to fit into her designer dress. Karen ran a small hairdressing business, called Karen's Kuts. She had two staff members: another hairdresser, and receptionist/cleaner. Neither of them were as competent as she wanted, but she'd had a succession of employees, and absolutely none of them had ever been competent. It was the bane of her life that no-one seemed to share her high standards.

Karen's morning had started badly. She was out of coffee. Why had she forgotten to pick some up? It couldn't have been her fault. Surely someone had distracted her at the supermarket, made her forget she needed coffee.

Karen's Kuts opened at ten am. It was nine. She had time to pick up a magazine, and go and read it in the coffee shop next door to her shop. She would sip her coffee slowly, relax and read until five to ten, then come back and open the hairdressing shop.

There was a line at the coffee shop. Why were there so many people, she wondered. Didn't any of these layabouts have jobs to go to? By the time she reached the front of the line, it was a quarter past nine. Her time to relax and read with her coffee had been diminished by all these useless people.

There in front of her, was the dumbest-looking barista on the planet: a young woman with a name tag which said "Linda".

"Good morning what can I get for you?" Linda said in an overly-enthusiastic voice.

"I'll have a large cappuccino, with extra chocolate on top, not too much foam, to have here."

The girl repeated her order in that overly-enthusiastic voice. Then she said, "I'm afraid we've been rushed this morning. We're out of china mugs. Is a takeaway cup OK? Otherwise we can get you a medium in a have here cup."

"No. I want a large cappuccino in a have here cup. That's not unreasonable. If you can't manage that, get me someone who can."

A second barista, a boy in his late teens, looked over from the coffee maker and asked: "Is there a problem?"

"I want a large cappuccino, and this stupid idiot can't even take my order without messing it up."

"Large cappuccino it is then," he said, almost as brightly as the girl had.

Karen paid, found a seat and began to read her magazine. A couple of minutes later, that inane Linda appeared and put a coffee on the table in front of her. It was in a takeaway cup.

Karen screeched. She stood up, picked up the coffee and threw it at Linda. The lid came off and the girl was covered in hot coffee.

Karen yelled: "Of all the stupid, incompetent, ignorant, waste of space people I have ever met, you are the worst!"

As she stalked out of the coffee shop, she heard Linda say, "May the rest of your day be as nice as you are."

Karen spun around in the doorway and demanded to know what that was supposed to mean.

"Oh it was just a thing my mother used to say. It's kind of a blessing, I think," Linda said, standing there, coffee dripping from her hair and clothes, looking every bit as useless as she was.

Karen turned back to the door and left, as Linda said under her breath. "Or maybe it's a curse."

As Karen exited the building, a pigeon flying overhead deposited a spectacularly large dropping on her head. Someone threw a lighted cigarette butt out of a passing car, which bizarrely landed in the pocket of her expensive suit. The suit jacket caught fire until she beat it with her hands.

With hands slightly burnt, hair befouled, and a smouldering hole in the pocket of her expensive jacket, she opened the door of her hairdressing salon.

She turned on the computer to check her bookings for the day, but it emitted puff of smoke, made a sizzling sound and stopped.

The phone rang. It was her other hairdresser, to say she was sick of Karen's bullying and she quit. Karen yelled at her through the phone, as her receptionist walked in the door.

Hearing what the conversation was, the receptionist said, "You know what? I've had a gut full of this. I'm out too."

Karen washed her hair in one of the sinks, and spilled shampoo on the floor. She wasn't as careful with styling and drying as she usually was, and her usually perfect hair was a mess.

One customer after another called to cancel their appointments. A couple came in, saw the state Karen was in and left.

Karen yelled at all of the people who missed appointments, ensuring they would never come back.

She paced around her shop like a caged tiger, stepped in the shampoo she'd spilled earlier and fell face-first on the floor, splitting her lip and breaking a tooth.

She realised the cause of all this was that weird blessing thing Linda at the coffee shop had said to her. She went back there.

121

Neither the baristas from earlier were behind the counter. Karen shouted: "Where's Linda?"

"She was on early today. She's gone home," the woman behind the counter said.

"I want her phone number, and her address!"

"I'm sorry, I can't give out employee's personal information."

Karen began to scream. She yelled her demand at the barista. She ranted. She raved.

I'm sorry to say dear Reader, Karen in her dishevelled state, yelling incomprehensible things, led everyone who witnessed this incident to believe she had some severe mental illness.

The barista who was not directly being yelled at called the police.

Now, dear Reader, Karen is spending the night in a nice, secure hospital ward. As for Linda, well, she's at home snuggled up with her cat, and a nice cup of cocoa, studying her mother's grimoire.

Whisper

I invite you dear Reader to get comfortable, settle in, while I tell you the strange tale of Christine, who got sick of seeing criminals get the better of justice.

Christine was a young journalist, working in her first job out of college. She covered the courts for her regional newspaper.

She sat to the side of the courtroom, and made her shorthand notes as the real-life legal drama played out.

At first, she'd enjoyed the work. She found the legal arguments interesting, and was keen to learn more about human nature.

As time went on, she became more and more disillusioned.

Following the rules of the court sometimes got in the way of truth, and some people clearly told lies.

Beyond that, from her vantage point as observer, rather than participant in the system, she noticed there seemed to be an unknowing bias. All of the solicitors and the magistrates in the lower court, and the barristers and the judges for the upper court were all men, and they were all white men.

Christine noticed that white men seemed to have a much easier time in court than other people. Aboriginal people seemed to get the worst penalties. Women of any race didn't seem to fare much better.

Christine confided her concerns to her Aunt, whom she lived with.

Her Aunt said, "If it's unfair, you know how to make it fairer."

Christine said, "I couldn't interfere, not in the legal system. That would be wrong."

"Is what you've seen happening right?"

So, dear Reader, Christine thought about what her Aunt had said, and about the responsibility that came with her family's gift.

That day there was a strange case on in court.

The case was Smith versus Mercer. A man, Edward Smith, was suing a work colleague, Julia Mercer, for defamation, because she had complained to their employer about him assaulting her at work.

Legal arguments took most of the morning. Then Smith began giving his evidence. He was arrogant, and denied any wrongdoing. He admitted what he'd done, but claimed it was consensual.

Mercer, sitting beside her lawyer, put her face in her hands, and sobbed. Her lawyer, in a loud whisper, told her to be quiet.

Christine could see Smith was lying. She could also see that the all of the men in the courtroom were sympathetic to his lies.

The judge interrupted his evidence to announce it was time to break for lunch.

Leaving the courtroom, Christine found herself walking beside Smith.

She whispered, "Tell the truth, only the truth, always the truth."

She walked a little faster, caught up to first on lawyer, then the other, and to each, she whispered, "Be fair, be honest, be just. Always be fair, always be honest, always be just."

His Honour was harder to get to, as he took lunch in his chambers.

Christine waited outside his door, and listened. When she was sure she could hear someone near the other side of the door, she whispered, "Seek the truth with all honesty. Treat all people as equal. Be blind to status, or gender or race. Be just, always be just."

She went to get her own lunch, hoping that she'd whispered to the judge, rather than just his clerk.

When court resumed, there seemed to be a different tone to the whole thing.

Mercer's lawyer was cross-examining, Smith. As soon as he began to ask questions, Smith, in the witness box, admitted that everything said about him had been true. There had been no consent, Mercer had struggled and fought against him. He had brought this court action to intimidate her, after she'd made the complaint. He wanted to show her how little power a woman could have.

Christine smiled a little. Some women did have power.

Mercer gave her evidence. Her lawyer simply asked her to tell her story, which she did, haltingly, through tears.

Ordinarily, Smith's lawyer would have questioned her aggressively, yelling at times, but he asked no questions, not after his own client had already admitted to being in the wrong.

His Honour found in favour of Mercer, and ordered costs against Smith. In the light of Smith's admissions, he had no other choice.

As they left the courtroom, Christine approached Ms Mercer. She asked: "Are you OK?"

"I am now," the woman said. "When I came in here this morning, and it seemed his lawyer and my lawyer were both friends, and they were both happily chatting with him, I was scared. I thought I really was in trouble."

"Yeah, it looked that way to me too."

"But why should I have to put up with being assaulted, and then being sued over it?"

"You shouldn't. No-one should. Luckily this time the system worked. It's just a pity it got this far."

"Did it seem to you that everything was different after lunch?"

"It did a bit."

"Like they'd all grown a conscience?"

"Maybe they did."

So dear Reader, we leave Christine, who has seen justice done, and who will take her Aunt's advice in future, and whisper carefully and selectively. She's always careful of her own biases and only asks for truth, justice, and fairness, not for any specific outcome she believes is appropriate.

Practical Jokes

I invite you, dear Reader, to get comfortable. Settle in while I tell you the strange tale of Francine, who'd had enough of her little brother's insensitive practical jokes.

Fran was a fifteen year old high school student. She was studious, intelligent, responsible, and kind. She was also an introvert, who was embarrassed easily. Her ten year old brother, Chris, was outgoing, seemingly charming, made friends easily, and was also a cruel child who had never suffered consequences for his actions.

Chris had discovered practical jokes. It started small. He would hide behind doorways and jump out at Fran. He would put rubber snakes or spiders in her school bag.

Whenever Fran complained to her parents she would be told, "Boys will be boys."

The only adult in Fran's life who seemed concerned about her feelings was her Aunt Judy, her father's sister. Judy was a single, childless, woman, who ran her own very successful business.

At a family barbecue, Chris grabbed a handful of dirt, threw it in Fran's plate, and yelled, "Joke!" He ran away laughing.

Fran burst into tears. Judy put an arm around her, then glared at her brother and sister-in-law.

She asked, "Are you doing anything about this? Anything? Max? Jenny?"

Fran's mother said, "She can eat something else when we get home. Missing a meal is no big deal."

Judy was shocked, "How about consequences for Chris?"

Jenny answered, "Oh well. You know, boys will be boys. There's nothing anyone can do about it."

Judy replied, "There are things you could do about it. You could raise your kid to not be an insensitive jerk."

Fran's parents were outraged. Jenny yelled, "What would you know about it? You've never raised a child!"

The barbecue broke up quickly, but while they were packing up, Judy pulled Fran aside, to ask how bad things were at home. Fran's answer bothered her a great deal.

"If you ever need anything, call me. If you want to move in with me as soon as you turn eighteen, you are welcome to. I'd take you with me now, but since you're still legally a child, that would count as kidnapping. If you want, I'll try to talk to them again when they've calmed down. I don't think I can prove what's happening to Children's Services, or I'd go to them. Any time you're scared, if you can do it without getting caught, use your phone to record what's going on."

The next day, Jenny bought Chris a gift to compensate for the trauma of all the adults yelling at the barbecue. It was a book, titled "Practical Jokes for Kids."

Fran asked, "Why would you do that?"

Her mother said, "It's important to support a young boy's interests."

"Out of curiosity, do you know what my interests are?"

"Oh, cooking, babysitting, usual teenage girl things."

"No. None of that is true."

"You're never satisfied with anything, always got to find something to complain about. I wish you wouldn't throw these tantrums."

That was the end of the conversation.

Later that day, when Fran went to use the toilet, something was very wrong. Fran didn't realise it until urine flowed over the side of the toilet, over the floor, over her skirt and underwear, and over her feet. She screamed. Then she saw there was plastic wrap between the seat and the toilet itself.

Dripping urine, she rushed to her mother to complain.

Her mother yelled at her to clean that up before her father got home.

So, Fran cleaned, showered, and washed her clothes. Then she called her aunt and told her about it.

Judy said, "I'm making a note of this, with the date and time, and Jenny's response. This is called evidence. I won't tell you to keep a diary there, because someone might find it, but I will keep it I spoke to a client of mine who works in the Children's Services Department. She said keeping evidence will help if we need to get you out of there. Call me or message me any time anything like this happens. It doesn't feel like it, but ultimately this will give you power over your life."

The next morning, when Fran got dressed, she found herself incredibly itchy. A look in her underwear drawer showed loose powder through all of her underwear, and a torn sachet labelled "itching powder" in the drawer. Fran showered, and put back on the underwear from the previous night.

This time, she set her phone to record audio, before she complained to her mother.

Jenny said, "Well, you'll have to wash all your clothes after school, and clean the drawer. You're perfectly capable of doing that. Eat your breakfast. You've been mucking around so long you're running late to walk Chris to school."

Fran hadn't stopped the recording. She sat down to eat her cereal. When she put her spoon in, a toy frog jumped out at her face. She screamed and jumped, knocking the bowl over.

Her father put down his morning newspaper, and said loudly. "That is enough! Francine, stop the histrionics now! And clean up your mess!"

129

Fran, still shaking, tried to explain what happened.

Max replied, "I don't want excuses. I want you to be quiet and clean up the mess you made."

It was only after she had left the house, that Fran remembered her phone was still recording. When she got to school, she sent the recording to her aunt, attached to an email detailing the whole morning's trauma.

At lunchtime, Fran sat with her friend, Beatrix.

Fran said, "Trix, it just keeps getting worse and worse. Mum and Dad just don't know what it's like to be the target of this stuff."

Beatrix replied, "Maybe it's time they found out. You have time before they get home from work, don't you? You could do all the same things to them, let them think Chris has decided to trick them now. Maybe then they'd stop him."

"I threw out the frog when I cleaned up the dining table, and I don't have itching powder. I have to take Chris home from school, so he'd know what I was doing if I stopped at the comic shop. That's where he gets his stuff. Anyway, I have to help him with his homework, which means I have to do it because he won't, and I have to cook dinner."

Her friend smiled, then laid out the plan of how they'd deal with it.

That afternoon, when Fran went next door to the primary school to get Chris, his teacher approached her. The teacher, Mrs Adamson, handed her a piece of folded paper. Fran unfolded it, and saw a pencil drawing of a woman with a knife in her stomach, and intestines pouring out. Written beside the woman, in Chris' handwriting, was, "Mrs Adamson."

The teacher said, "I'd like to talk to your parents about this, can you ask them to contact me?"

The gross drawing gave Fran an idea. She said, "I'll tell them, but they don't ever really do much about his behaviour."

"Believe me, I've noticed. You were always such a great student. I don't understand how your parents could raise two such completely different children."

At home, Fran said to Chris, "I don't have the energy to fight over you doing your homework. Leave it on the dining table for me and I'll take care of it. Just go and play your games."

Cassie began to cut up vegetables for dinner.

When she was sure Chris was too engrossed in his console game to notice anything, she took the plastic wrap from the kitchen, and went to her parent's ensuite. She put plastic over the toilet the way Chris had done in their shared bathroom.

Then she took the awful drawing Chris had done. She carefully erased Mrs Adamson's name, and in her best imitation of Chris' handwriting, honed over years of doing his homework, she wrote, "Mum." She left it on her mother's dressing table.

She returned to the kitchen and put the vegetables, some washed lentils and rice, and stock in a saucepan to make soup.

Then she mixed garlic and butter together, cut a stick of French bread, and spread it with the garlic butter, wrapped it in foil, and placed it in the oven. She would turn the oven on closer to time for dinner.

A text message came from Trix. It said, "Back door."

Both girls knew Fran wasn't allowed to have friends over, so Fran double-checked Chris was still lost in his game before quietly going to the door.

Trix handed over a jumping frog and a sachet labelled "itching powder."

Fran went back to her parents' room, and sprinkled the powder through her father's underwear drawer, leaving the packet in the drawer, just as Chris had done.

131

She checked the soup was simmering nicely, and set the table.

When her parents arrived home, she turned on the oven, and told them dinner would be ready in fifteen minutes.

Her father followed his regular routine, and took a book to read on the toilet for ten minutes. This time, he did not stay there for ten minutes before Fran heard the yell, then heard her parents' shower running.

Her father was clearly angry as he came downstairs, scratching his private area.

Her mother appeared at the table, with mascara running. She'd clearly been crying.

Fran had served the soup and garlic bread. She sat down to dinner, acting as if she'd no idea anything strange was happening. She had her phone in her school uniform pocket, recording.

Innocently, she said, "Mrs Adamson said she wants to talk to one of you about Chris."

Her mother said, "What about?"

Fran said, "Something about drawings. She wants to talk to you or Dad, not me."

A frog jumped out of Jenny's soup at her, causing her to scream, jump, and knock over her soup bowl.

"That is more than enough!" Max roared, as he scratched himself. "These jokes have to stop!"

Chris looked confused.

Max yelled at Fran, "You were meant to be looking after him! How could you let him do this?"

Cassie said, "Well, Mum always just says, 'Boys will be boys.' She says there's nothing that can be done about it."

"I'm not talking to your mother! I'm talking to you! You were responsible for him all afternoon! What were you doing?"

132

"I was doing his homework, cooking dinner, doing the laundry. You know, basic parental responsibilities. I haven't even had time for my own homework. If you want me to discipline him as well, you need to back me up doing that. You need to give him consequences for his actions. I can't control him if I don't have the authority to do it. I'm not his parent."

"How dare you talk to me like that? I am your father! You will respect me!"

"Why? What have you done to deserve it?"

"That's it! Get out of my house now, and don't come back!"

Without saying anything more, Fran got up from the table and started walking towards the front door.

Her mother said, "What do you think you're doing?"

Fran answered, "I'm doing what Dad told me to do."

Outside, she called Judy and told her she'd been thrown out of the house.

Judy picked her up. She listened to the recording, and had Fran send it to her.

On the way to Judy's home they stopped at the police station. Judy told them her niece had been thrown out of the family home, and they'd like a police escort to go the next morning to collect her clothes and personal belongings. She played the recording, then offered to provide all of Francine's evidence of mistreatment.

The next day, a police officer and a Children's Services caseworker accompanied Judy and Fran to the home to collect Fran's possessions.

The Children's Services caseworker advised Max and Jenny that an investigation was being started into their family.

"You can't take Francine away from us," Jenny said. "We need her to look after Chris."

The caseworker replied, "Your husband already threw Francine out. We've approved Judy as an emergency placement, and I believe that will quickly become a permanent placement. We're investigating whether this is an appropriate place for Chris to live, and whether we need to work with your family to improve things here."

"Chris? Of course this is an appropriate place for him. This is his home."

"What kind of consequence does he experience for misbehaviour?"

"He's a boy! You know that boys will be boys."

"So that's no consequences, is it? We'll be in touch."

So, dear Reader, we leave Francine. She's much happier now that she only has to do a reasonable amount of chores, and isn't having horrible "jokes" played on her constantly. She's even allowed to see her friend after school. Her parents, at last, are having to learn how to be parents, and Chris has heard the word "no" for the first time in his life. What's that, dear Reader? I always include magic in my tales, and you didn't see it this time? This was a rare and special magic. In a world of people being horrible to her, a young woman claimed her own power.

Fairy Godmother

I invite you, dear Reader, to get comfortable. Settle in while I tell you the strange tale of Katrina, who just wanted to go to her high school formal.

Kat had saved all of her money from her part time job for months, to buy her ticket and her dress for the formal. She'd even hired a limousine.

Her father, Jeffrey, was away for work. He often was. They lived in a very nice house, with lots of luxuries, because of the work he did. He'd messaged Kat to tell her to have a great night, and to ask her to send him a photo of her dressed up for the outing.

When Kat asked her step-mother Michelle to take the photo, she was surprised to see Michelle also dressed up.

Michelle took the photo, with Kat's phone, then sent the photo to Jeffrey. She didn't give the phone back.

She then told Kat, that she, Michelle had to go out. Kat would have to stay home to look after her step-brother Jayden. Since Kat wouldn't need that limo after all, and it was too late to cancel, Michelle would use it. She finished the speech with, "If you want to continue living here through uni, your father will not hear anything about this. As far as he's concerned, you've gone to the formal, and had a great night. Do you understand me?"

Knowing university would be much harder if she had to live away from home, Kat tearfully nodded.

Michelle gave the phone back.

The limo came, Michelle got in, and it drove away.

Kat threw frozen chips and nuggets into the air fryer for Jayden's dinner. She didn't have the will to do anything for herself.

She sat and cried.

Suddenly, the kitchen was filled with coloured sparks, and a woman appeared. She was tall and thin, wearing a glimmering dress and white wings. In one hand, she held a pink and white magic wand, and in the other a glass of sparkling wine.

"Cheer up, kid, it can't be that bad," the woman said.

"Oh yes it can. My step-mother's out, probably with a boyfriend. My father's away and doesn't know what's going on. And I'm missing my formal, when I've worked for six months just to afford it."

"This formal, you don't just want to go because of some boy, do you?"

"No. It's a special night out with my high school friends, before we all go our seperate ways for uni. It's a rite of passage, and I've worked hard for it. I've earned it."

"Oh, that's all right then. I did one of those wanting to impress a boy ones once. Total disaster. The boy was so clueless he couldn't even recognise her without her make-up on, had to identify her by her shoe. Utterly ridiculous. She was a smart kid, too, and a hard worker. She could have done so much better. Now you. You're smart, you work hard, and you know what you're worth. You're much better off. So let's get you to that ball. I mean the formal."

"How? I've got to stay here and look after the gremlin." Kat pointed to Jayden, who was at that moment crashing his toy cars into an expensive vase that had belonged to Kat's deceased mother.

The woman waved her wand, and in a cloud of coloured sparks, she changed shape, and now looked like Kat. She said, "I'll stay here like, you know. I can be like, a teenager, like, you know."

"I don't talk like that. No-one I know talks like that. Can you just talk normally?"

136

"If you insist. I was just getting into the part."

"Michelle took my ride. I could catch a bus, but wouldn't make it in time."

The woman approached Jayden. "Hey Jay, do you mind if I borrow one of these cars? How about your Ken doll? We might have to put his head back on."

The woman who looked like Kat took the toys outside, and with another wave of the wand and another pile of sparks, the car became a limo, and the doll became a chauffeur.

Kat looked at it all. "Let me guess, it changes back at midnight?"

"That's right kid."

"So are you my fairy godmother or something."

"Something like that. Go have fun. Take what you've earned. While you're gone I'll watch the kid, and maybe I'll help someone else get what they've earned as well."

Kat went to the formal, caught up with her friends, danced, laughed and had fun. Occasionally during the night she wondered what the fairy godmother had meant by helping someone else get what they'd earned.

Back at the house, the fake Kat had fed Jayden, and then begun exploring the house.

She found Michelle's laptop. Passwords meant nothing to her, as her wand gave her any access she wanted. She smiled as she saw it was connected to Michelle's phone, and she had access to all of Michelle's text messages. Oh dear, there was a glitch in the computer, and a copy of all those messages between Michelle were forwarded to all of her contacts, including Jeffrey.

At the formal, Kat heard a message alert on her phone, took it out of her phone and saw the stream of messages. She smiled. Someone really was going to get what they deserved.

They also received an extra file, magically created. It contained video of all the horrible things Michelle had said and done to Kat in the year since Michelle and Jeffrey had been married. All the threats to throw Kat out. The last thing on the file was Michelle telling Kat she couldn't go to the formal, and taking the limo ride Kat had paid for. At the end of that file, was Michelle saying she was sorry, her conscience had got the better of her, and she felt she had to confess. The fairy godmother was very proud of that last special touch.

Jayden had finished eating and was back to running toy cars into expensive objects.

Fake Kat said to him, "Is there something more constructive you could be doing? Reading a book? Getting ready for bed? Graffiti-ing the neighbourhood? Fire bombing a police station? What's your bed-time anyway?"

"No bed-time for me. No rules for me. Mum says I can do what I want."

"I can see why babysitting you makes Kat cry."

"Mum says its funny when Kat cries." He hit a car into a crystal owl ornament, shattering it.

The fairy godmother waved the wand, repairing the owl. "Your Mum's going to do a lot of crying soon. Should be really funny. Get ready for lots of laughs."

"I want my toys back. The ones you let Kat take."

"They'll be back tonight. You've got plenty."

"But these ones are little. You made the other ones big."

"Very observant of you. OK. Let's make something big. What's this over here? Do you want this big?"

"Dinosaur!" Jayden squealed.

"We might have to take it outside to make it big."

Jayden excitedly carried the tyrannosaurus to the back yard.

The fairy godmother calculated that it would have to be a quarter size to be able to fit in the space, the sparks filled the air, and a suddenly alive plastic dinosaur looked around and roared. It was in a bad mood, having been stomped on, shoved in the toilet, chewed, smashed head-first into the tv, and now brought to life without its consent.

It saw the author of its many degradations, roared again, and gave chase. The fairy godmother had not given it much speed so, hampered, the dinosaur was unable to catch its quarry. She allowed the chase to continue until she judged the child to be exhausted, and then turned the tyrannosaurus back to plastic.

"Time to get ready for bed now?" She asked.

Jayden agreed, and went compliantly to bathe and put on his pyjamas.

He was asleep by the time Kat got home.

Not long after that, Michelle arrived. She was furious.

Michelle ran into the lounge room, where Kat was sitting, and yelled at her, "What did you do?"

The fairy godmother, still looking like Kat entered from the kitchen with two cups of hot chocolate. "She went to the formal, just as she worked for, earned, and deserved," the fairy godmother said. Then, with a wave of her want she turned herself back to her former appearance.

Michelle turned her confused anger to her and demanded, "Who the hell are you?"

"I'm the one who watched your badly-raised brat. Oh, and I did a little snooping on your computer as well."

Michelle turned to Kat, "Katrina who is this woman? Did you let her in here? Did you leave her alone with my precious boy? Where is he anyway?"

Kat shook her head. She said, "I didn't invite her. She just came. And yes, I did leave her with Jayden. She's an adult,

139

and I'm not one for a couple of months yet. I thought she'd be a more responsible carer than me. As for where he is, since his snoring is so loud, I would guess he actually went to bed, because, again, an adult babysitter managed to do what I never can, and got him to go."

Michelle rushed to Jayden's bedroom, and shook him awake to ask him if anything bad had happened to him. He sleepily told her about having fun playing with a big dinosaur in the yard.

Michelle came back to the lounge room to find Kat and the fairy godmother chatting about the formal, and sipping their hot chocolate, as if the whole evening had been the most normal thing in the world.

The fairy godmother smiled sweetly at Michelle, and said, "A little bit of advice for you. Jeffrey's going to be a tad upset when he gets through reading absolutely everything. You and your little terror really should be gone by the time he gets back. Cheating on him the whole time you were married, and texting to your boyfriend about how much money you're getting from Jeffrey really isn't a good look. It's such a good thing he's got a signed prenup."

"I never signed a prenup!"

"Funny thing that, though. You see, there's a signed prenup in Jeffrey's papers, and another copy in his solicitor's safe, and both of them clearly remember you signing it. It really is your signature, signed and witnessed. Magic, you see, is very good for helping people get what they really truly earned. What you earned, was nothing."

"So what are you? Katrina's fairy godmother or something?"

"Oh no Michelle! I'm *your* fairy godmother. It's my job to make sure you get exactly what you deserve, and if, along the way, I can set a few injustices right, I'll do that, too. Now, I'm off, but I'll be watching, so don't you dare retaliate against Kat for what I've done."

She disappeared in a shower of coloured sparks.

Kat finished her hot chocolate, and went to her room, ignoring the seething Michelle.

So, dear Reader, we leave Katrina, who is a little confused and greatly relieved to know the evil step-mother and annoying little step-brother won't be in her life much longer. The fairy godmother was right, she's a smart young woman, a hard worker, and does know her worth. She's going to do well in university, and in the rest of her life.

Bully

I invite you, dear Reader, to get comfortable. Settle in while I tell you the strange tale of Lucia, who found herself compelled to live with her school bully.

Lucia was sixteen, in grade eleven at school. For entire high school experience up until this point, she had suffered at the hands of a vicious bully Nathan.

He called her names, snatched her books and tore them, pulled her hair, made fun of her, and generally made her life unpleasant.

She had complained to the school multiple times, and asked them to implement their "zero tolerance on bullying policy". Sadly, she found that the school's tolerance for bullying was far from zero, as Nathan was the nephew of the Principal.

To make matters worse, when Lucia was in grade nine, her parents had separated, and when she was in grade ten they'd divorced.

The divorce had been brutal. Her father Roderick had discovered that by minimising the time his ex-wife Judith had custody of Lucia, he could minimise the amount of child support he paid. As he had a high-paying job, and Judith had a low-paying one, Roderick was able to hire a very expensive solicitor. So Lucia had to spend all week days and alternate weekends at her father's house, and only had one weekend per fortnight with her mother.

At her father's house, Lucia was mostly ignored, except to be given housework to do. Roderick simply didn't have time for her, and didn't have the interest in making time for her.

Her mother's house, however, was the opposite. Judith always made time for anything Lucia wanted. There was little money, but there was much love.

That, terrible as it is, is just background, dear Reader. Now we take you to the story, which as mentioned earlier, is set when Lucia was sixteen.

One Sunday night, when Lucia returned to her father's house, she discovered two people had moved in during her absence.

Roderick introduced his girlfriend Janelle, and her son, Nathan. It was, of course the same Nathan who had made so much of her life miserable at school.

Since Nathan would live there all of the time, and Lucia was away two nights per fortnight, her father and his girlfriend had decided it was only fair that Nathan had his choice of bedroom. Of course, he had chosen Lucia's room. All of her clothes and other possessions had been shoved haphazardly in the tiny room that had been used for storage. Roderick told her, they still needed storage space, so she would have to share the room with the hardly-used suitcases, boxes of old odds and ends, toolboxes, and other detritus junk rooms collected.

While carefully trying to put her things away, Lucia discovered her books were all wet. The smell suggested someone had urinated on them. She complained to her father, who told her to just deal with it, and not ruin this new relationship for him.

She threw her beloved books out, not knowing what else to do with them.

Nathan's bullying now escalated at school and continued at home. The school principal, and her father both ignored it. When Lucia complained to Janelle, she said, "You have to make allowances for high spirits."

On her next visit to her mother's house, Lucia begged to not be sent back.

Judith called Roderick and asked to change the custody agreement. She offered to let him off paying child support completely, if Lucia could stay at her house. Roderick, seeing a way to hurt Judith, insisted he was following the court's order to the letter, and he would bring court action against her if she disobeyed.

It seemed, dear Reader, that Lucia would have to live with her bully until she reached adulthood. Fortunately, her mother had access to resources that Roderick knew nothing about.

Judith said to Lucia, "I will take this back to court, and you're old enough that the court might consider what you want. I know your father will bring his high-powered lawyer back, and I can't afford to match that. So I think, maybe we should even things up a little. I didn't want to do this, but I can't leave you in that situation."

Lucia, confused, asked, "What do you mean?"

"Well, you know I inherited this house from my grandmother; and you know I didn't exactly get on with her, but I was the only family she had. My grandmother had a secret, which I've spent my whole life trying to live down. Now, though, I think we need to take advantage of it."

"What kind of secret?"

Judith walked over to the bookshelf that covered an entire wall of the lounge room. She pulled out one of the books and pressed a button behind it.

Being a prolific Reader, Lucia had read of rooms behind book cases, and secret passageways, but she'd never imagined they were real, or in her mother's house.

On the other side of the book case was a narrow stairway, made of stone, with stone walls close on either side of it. There was no light source, but it wasn't dark, rather the stones themselves seemed to emit as soft light.

"Stay with me, and don't touch anything unless I tell you to," Judith said.

144

Lucia nodded mutely, and carefully followed her mother down the steep steps.

At the bottom, there was a large room, probably as large as the entire floor of the house above. The walls were stone, and it was lit with the same soft light as the stairway had been.

In the centre of the room was a large, heavy, wooden table. Three of the walls were lined with shelves, some of which contained books, but most contained glass jars of powders and liquids, with names written on them. Lucia read words like; "wolfsbane", and "arsenic", and decided her mother was right to tell her not to touch anything.

The fourth wall had a large open fireplace. Lucia wondered where smoke from the fire would go, as the house above had no chimney. Further along the wall, a copper pipe stuck out between the rocks, and water slowly dripped from it, landing in a drain below.

Judith said, "This was my grandmother's work room, and her mother's as well. It would have been my mother's if she hadn't died having me, and mine if I hadn't refused to use the arts my grandmother taught me."

"Why did you refuse?"

"Magic sounds great in books and movies. In the real world, well, there's a saying that power corrupts. Magical power can be just as corrupting as political or economic power. Not only that, but it makes people scared when they are aware of it, and scared people act irrationally. That's why we had witch hunts."

"So you wouldn't normally just use this? Even if it made your life easier?"

"No, not normally. This isn't normal. We're not going to do any harm, we're just going to persuade your father to do what's right. Do you understand?"

Lucia nodded.

Her mother continued, "If you look at the shelves around the room, you will see a lot of things that could easily kill someone. We are not going to use any of those things. If you should decide you want to learn about the family heritage, I will teach you about them, because you have the right to know who you are. You are old enough now to understand."

Lucia nodded again. She wanted to speak, but didn't know what to say. How could she have not known about any of this?

Judith showed Lucia a very old leather-bound book, with yellowing paper. It had "Grimoire" written on the cover.

"This is our family Grimoire," Judith said. "There are many other books of spells on the shelves, but this is the one which records favourites of family members, or ones that our ancestors developed themselves."

Lucia nodded again, still too overwhelmed with everything to ask the million questions running around her brain.

Judith carefully turned the pages of the old book. Then she stood the book on a stand on the table.

Lucia looked at the page, and was surprised it was in English. She said, "I thought it would be in Latin, or something like that."

Judith smiled. "Some of the books on the shelves are in dead languages like Latin, but a Grimoire is almost always in the language commonly used by the people who wrote in it. It's like a personal notebook, but it gets passed from mother to daughter. So first, we need wax. We're tripling the recipe for this, because there's three people we want to affect."

Judith took a large box of beeswax, and some old fashioned scales from a shelf, and carefully weighed three times the recipe on the page of the Grimoire. She put the wax in a large black cauldron. Then she took other ingredients from the shelves, and weighed them, and added them.

She got Lucia to help her carry the cauldron, and hang it on a hook over the fireplace. The fire seemed to light itself.

"We only want to soften the wax, not completely melt it, so this won't take long," Judith said.

Lucia watched the fire with wonder, noticing that the flames did not seem to actually burn the wood.

It was not long before Judith said it was hot enough, and they both put on heavy gloves to lift the pot, carry it to the table, and dump the contents on the table top.

Judith said, "Grab a third of it, and form it into a human shape. It doesn't have to be perfect, or even particularly good. Just head, body arms and legs."

Lucia did as she was told, while Judith used the other two thirds of the wax mix to make two more models. She had clearly done it before.

Judith scraped the last of the wax residue from the pot, squashed it into a ball, took another herb from a jar, and added a couple of flakes to the wax ball. She opened a box on another shelf, and took a gold locket on a chain from it. She pressed the wax into the locket, then pressed a small dried flower into the wax.

"That's all we can do for now," Judith said. "Now I need you to do something. I need some part of each of them, Roderick, Janelle and Nathan. It can be a strand of hair pulled from a brush or comb, a nail clipping taken from the bin, anything that was once a part of each of them. I will be waiting at your school gate on Monday afternoon, and you can pass them to me then. I want you to wear the locket at all times. Once I've added the body parts to each of the models, every time they consider doing something that is harmful to you, they will feel sick. Nothing very bad will happen to them, not unless they do something extremely bad to you. This is a balancing spell. Whatever they do to you will be countered back to them, in a balance."

"So if Nathan pulls my hair?"

"He'll probably have a small bout of diarrhoea, or throw up."

"And if Dad refuses to let you have custody?"

"It won't be fatal, but then again, it won't be pleasant either."

When Lucia went back to her father's house on Sunday night, she was upset to discover most of her clothes had been cut or torn. She cried for a few minutes, before realising that this was exactly the kind of thing that would have consequences very soon.

While collecting the family's dirty clothes to wash, she checked brushes and combs. She carefully wrapped each hair in paper, noting whose it was.

She didn't even complain about the damage to her clothes. She had one clean, uncut, uniform for school the next day, and by the next night things would start to change.

After school on Monday, she went to the gate to pass the papers containing the hairs to her mother. Judith opened the shopping bag she was carrying. All three wax models were in it. She pressed a hair into each one. As a hair was pressed into each, they changed shape, looking more like the people they represented. As both Judith and Lucia were looking at the wax models in the bag, neither was aware of Nathan.

He walked up behind Lucia and said, "You're not supposed to see her now. I'm telling on you." Then he doubled over, grasping his stomach. There was a loud grumbling noise, and the air around him was filled with a noxious smell. Other students leaving the school grounds groaned and laughed, some whispered and pointed.

Lucia and Judith couldn't help laughing as well. Nathan yelled, and then punched Lucia. There was another ominous grumble, and quite obviously Nathan emitted more than gas.

148

He walked awkwardly back to the school to try to clean himself up, while other students laughed and pointed.

Judith placed a cool hand on the side of Lucia's face, where she had been punched. Lucia suddenly realised why her mother's touch had always been enough to soothe minor hurts and injuries.

"I'll see you soon," Judith said.

"Sure Mum, see you soon," Lucia responded with a smile.

Lucia practically skipped to her father's house.

She started doing housework, and cooking dinner. Eventually Nathan came home, wearing some ill-fitting shorts that must have come from the school's lost property box. He had his fouled shorts and underwear in a plastic bag.

"Wash these," he said, thrusting the bag at Lucia. His stomach groaned.

"I don't think so," Lucia answered. "You dirtied it, you clean it. It's about time you learned."

That was when Janelle arrived.

Lucia immediately complained that someone had cut and torn all her clothes while she was away for the weekend.

Janelle looked at her a moment and said, "Tough. I guess you'll have to learn how to mend."

Janelle's stomach rumbled, and she emitted a massive toot of foul-smelling gas.

"So you're not going to punish Nathan?" Lucia asked.

"What? No!" Janelle squeaked as she ran for the bathroom.

"What are you going to do about this?" Nathan demanded, once more shoving the plastic bag in Lucia's face. Then he too ran for the bathroom, but as Janelle was already in there, fouled himself outside the door.

149

Lucia went back to preparing dinner. She was going to eat, even if no-one else did.

Janelle was lying down, and Nathan was crying in the shower when Roderick came home.

When Nathan eventually left the bathroom, Roderick entered. He found two sets of Nathan's befouled shorts and underwear spread all over the floor, and yelled for Nathan to come and clean up his mess.

Nathan yelled back, "Make Lucia do it!" Then he ran back, pushing Roderick out of the way, to get to the bathroom.

"Gee Dad," Lucia said. "Maybe when you moved out of Mum's place, you should have got a house with two bathrooms. After all you can afford it. And thinking about what you can afford, Nathan ripped up all my clothes. Can you please buy me some new things?"

"Oh for God's sake, work it out. I'm not here to referee between the two of you," he grumbled, as he suddenly felt a piercing pain in his abdomen. He doubled up in pain.

"You must have whatever Nathan and Janelle have," Lucia said. "Oh dear. So do you want dinner? Does anyone want dinner?"

No-one, it seemed, wanted dinner. Lucia had a quiet meal on her own.

After dinner, the other three family members, looking paler, sat in the lounge room to watch tv.

"Can I please ask, Dad, why you won't let me live with Mum? None of you really want me here, do you?"

Suddenly all three were up and yelling at her, then racing each other for the bathroom.

Her father really should have invested in a house with more than one bathroom, Lucia reflected as they fought for the bathroom, made further mess, and yelled at each other.

When her father came back, Lucia asked again about going to her mother's house.

Roderick doubled over and began projectile vomiting over his own shoes, as he gasped out that he would not allow it.

Eventually, he accused Lucia of poisoning them all. To prove his point, he took Nathan and Janelle to hospital, where they all had tests, which proved they did not have food poisoning or any other kind of poisoning. An emergency room doctor suggested that perhaps they had all caught a virus, or otherwise they might need to have healthier diets, or had a little too much stress in their lives.

When they got home, they all avoided talking to Lucia. That was fine by her.

Over the next couple of days, whenever one of them yelled at her, refused her constant requests to go to her mother's house, or tried to put excess work onto her, got sick. It was worst for Nathan, who at school stole her pen, pulled her hair, and tried to start a rumour that she was dating a thirty year old drug dealer. Each of these activities led to him having embarrassing bouts of the illness he'd seemed to contract recently.

Eventually, Janelle said to Lucia, "You're causing this aren't you?"

As Janelle grasped her stomach, Lucia asked, "What if I am? Maybe it would be best for you if I weren't here? Maybe you should persuade Dad to send me to my mother's house to live, so you're all safe from me."

Janelle said, "I'm not letting her win, or you. Just stop it." She emitted a particularly loud and fragrant cloud of gas.

"But you see, I can't," Lucia said. "I'm not actually controlling it. But it does seem to be related to how you all treat me, doesn't it? I wonder what that could mean?"

After a week, Roderick finally gave in. Lucia was sent to live with her mother. Roderick even applied to the court to change the custody agreement, and paid the increased child support, under the condition that Lucia was never to come to his house again.

Lucia and Judith were both quite happy to comply with that condition.

So, dear Reader, we leave Lucia, happily learning everything her mother can teach her about magic. She's more than happy to accept her mother's conditions that it only ever be used as a last resort, and that it should only be used for justice, never spite. Lucia still wears her magic locket, just in case.

Wand

I invite you, dear Reader, to get comfortable. Settle in as I tell you the strange tale of Jessica, who inherited something she never expected.

Jessica had been vaguely aware that her mother's Aunt Gerda existed, but hadn't actually known her. The only thing her mother had ever told her was that Gerda was crazy, and had refused to do anything about her obvious mental illness.

Jessica's mother and grandmother had both cut crazy Gerda out of their lives, and no-one was really willing to say what she'd done to deserve it. Jessica had grown up only ever hearing the name whispered behind closed doors.

It came as a surprise, then, the day Jessica got home from work to see a long, thin, parcel beside her front door.

She took it inside and opened it to find, wrapped in bubble wrap, a wand such as a stage magician might use, and a letter from a solicitor.

The letter said, "In my capacity as executor for the estate of Gerda Zwillinger, I send you this object she has bequeathed to you, along with her explanatory letter."

Jessica was amused the lawyer had avoided putting "magic wand" in her official letter.

She turned to the explanatory letter her great aunt had written. It said, "My dear Jessica. I realise you don't know me and may not have even heard of me. That is to be expected for people like us. I saw at your birth that you shared my immense talent, so I am passing my wand to you. Your mother would not allow me to take charge of your training, so I realise you have much to learn. You will not be the first to be self trained. The key thing to remember is that the wand reads the practitioner's intent. Don't go waving it willy nilly, as anything could happen. Use a firm hand with a firm command in mind."

That was it. That was the entirety of her great aunt's message from beyond the grave.

She wondered if her mother had received anything.

Her mother wasn't keen on texting, so Jessica rang her.

Jessica's mother Agnes, was not amused with the idea of her aunt sending Jasmine a stage prop.

Jessica laughed, and said she thought it was sweet that the old woman had thought of her.

She toyed with the wand while she talked. Suddenly a huge cake appeared on the kitchen bench. She realised she'd been thinking of getting a snack, but that really shouldn't have meant a massive cake should materialise in her kitchen.

"Ah, Mum, I've got to go. But I really want to know more about Aunt Gerda, so can I come and visit tomorrow night?"

She barely heard her mother's "Yes," as she pressed the end call button. Jessica didn't know how long she just stood and stared at the cake. No matter how long she looked, it didn't seem any less real, any less *there*.

Eventually, she decided she may as well find out what magically conjured cake tasted like, and cut a slice. It was good. It was, in fact, the best cake she could ever remember tasting. Apparently her great aunt's wand did quality work.

She picked up the wand again, to inspect it closely. It seemed to be made of wood, was painted black, with white tips at both ends.

Her front doorbell rang. She opened the door to see Jamie. Of all the days to see her stalkerish ex! Jamie had been harassing her for over a year since they broke up. He waited outside her work, he dropped by the house, he messaged her on social media. She really wanted him to not be there, and suddenly he wasn't. Jessica looked down at the wand in her hand. Had she been pointing it at him? Did she need to point it to make it work? Where had Jamie gone? Had he ceased to exist? Did she kill him?

Dear Reader, I'm sure you can imagine just how disturbed Jessica was at this point. If she could do this, whatever she had done by accident, what could she do intentionally?

Jessica carefully, rewrapped the wand in the bubble wrap, and put it in a drawer in her bedroom. She firmly decided she would not wave it willy nilly, in fact she would not touch it at all, unless absolutely necessary.

The next day dragged by slowly, Jessica's mind was somewhere else. She didn't know how she managed to survive the slow work day. Why should she deal with the work day anyway? She had a magic wand at home that could give her everything she wanted.

After work, she went home, and got the wand, and the rest of the cake to take to her mother's house.

She made certain to put the wand down on a table there, before telling her mother everything that had happened.

Agnes, strangely, didn't seem surprised by any of it. She picked up the wand as if she was familiar with it, waved it at the cake and made the cake disappear.

"It's still as powerful as ever," she said.

Jessica, surprised, said: "I thought you said it was just a stage prop yesterday!"

"Yesterday, I didn't know you'd tried to use it. Well, now you know, Jess. Everyone in our family has this gift, some stronger than others. Most of us are smart enough to not use it. Aunt Gerda wasn't that smart. She threw herself into witchcraft. People noticed. She almost had the whole family killed. Witches still get killed, you know, just not officially or in public. People don't accept magic. They don't accept people who have power they don't have. If you have any sense, you'll

155

put that stupid thing away somewhere, and never think about it or use it again."

"And if I don't? Do I become this generation's crazy person who everyone pretends doesn't exist?"

Her mother was quiet a moment before saying, "No. No, I can't. I can't cut you out the way my mother and grandmother cut Gerda out. But I do warn you. Using that wand will only cause trouble. Do you even know where you sent Jamie?"

Jessica sighed, "No, I just wanted him gone. I don't know where gone was, or is. I wasn't planning to send him anywhere. It just happened."

"Well, given all of the possible places he could be, I might suggest you use the wand one more time. This time, think of an actual place you'd like him to go."

Jessica thought she'd like to actually see Jamie in jail, but realised that was a vindictive choice. Instead, she concentrated on Jamie being at his grandmother's house in the outback in another state. He could find his way home safely from there, but he wouldn't bother her for a while.

"Now wrap that thing up, so you don't accidentally touch it," her mother instructed.

"But what if we used it to get rich? Or to go on holiday?"

"To get things without working for them, you mean? Jess, you have to understand, that takes us back to the whole drawing attention, making people scared, and then making them dangerous, thing. Jamie stalking you was bad enough, although I'm sure he's not going to do that anymore. You don't want lots of people stalking you, wanting things from you, or wanting to harm you."

Jessica smiled, "Well, Jamie went to we don't know where, and now to his grandma's property in the middle of nowhere. He's going to have plenty of time to think before he gets home."

"So the wand?"

"I'll think carefully before using it."

"But you won't promise not to use it?"

"No, I won't."

"Then at least promise be careful."

"That, I will promise."

Rest assured, dear Reader, Jessica was very careful. She didn't simply create money, but she did advance in her career a little faster than others. Her house and garden did require maintenance, but nowhere near as much as anyone else's. Her way through life was just a little easier than it might have been.

Dinner Guests

I invite you dear Reader to get comfortable, settle in while I tell you the strange tale of Ellen who had uninvited dinner guests, and learned that hospitality can have its own rewards.

Things were difficult for Ellen. Her parents and her husband had all been killed in a car accident only a month earlier. She and her five year old twins Candice and Terrance had been in a second car, and been first on the scene of the the accident.

She and the children had moved from a rented house to the one she inherited from her parents, the house she had grown up in. It was on the outer edge of the city, bordering on a national park. Ellen had grown up taking walks in the forest with her parents.

Ellen was taking time off from work, while she tried to work out what life would be like now, how she and the children would get by. Candy and Terry seemed to be handling the situation better than her. Children were resilient.

She was writing a grocery list. She'd realised she'd left it too long, and the pantry and fridge were practically empty. Little things like grocery shopping hadn't seemed important anymore, but sooner or later, they had to be done.

Actually, big things hadn't seemed important anymore either. She had run out of bereavement leave, the last of her annual leave, and was now on unpaid leave, with bills, including three funerals needing to be paid soon.

The children were watching tv. Ellen had stopped limiting their screen time. It didn't seem to matter any more.

There was a knock at the door. Ellen wasn't expecting anyone.

Two men were there. They were huge, tall, and with muscle on muscle on muscle. One of the men said, "We are travellers, and have far to go. We will eat with you today."

Ellen's first thought was to slam the door in their faces, but something held her back. She remembered her mother hosting strangers during her childhood. Periodically strangers would come to the door, ask for a meal, and they would then be the family's dinner guests. Her mother had said such hospitality was important, but never gave a reason why. Ellen had a vague recollection of something in the Bible about people unknowingly hosting angels, but had know idea if that was why her mother had done this.

Recalling her mother, she told them, "I don't have much, but I'll share what I have."

She stepped back from the doorway, to let them in, and said, "Dinner will be a while, please, have a seat."

The two sat down in the lounge area, where the children were watching a typical show for five year olds, which had lots of music and dancing.

Ellen was confronted with the question of what to cook, when she'd allowed groceries to get so low.

She checked the freezer, hoping there might still be some chops or something in there. She was surprised to find the freezer somehow full. She took out packs of frozen filet steak, and defrosted them in the microwave.

She knew she had a couple of potatoes, perhaps mixed with whatever other vegetables were still in the crisper drawer of the fridge, they would be able to be stretch far enough. She opened the cupboard where the potatoes were stored on a rack, to find the rack was full of them.

Confused, Ellen checked the fridge, to find it full. She selected cobs of corn, green beans, mushrooms and red wine. When did she last buy red wine? How did any of that get there? She was increasingly confused.

She checked on the children, to find them dancing to a song on the television. The visitors were dancing with them. They were spinning and leaping in a way that should have caused vibrations on the old wooden floor and shaken whole house. Strangely, however, their feet seemed to barely touch the floorboards, as if gravity were optional for them.

Ellen returned to the kitchen. She remembered a sauce her mother made with mushrooms and red wine. She found the old exercise book her mother had written all her recipes in. In that, she found the recipe, and she made a meal reminiscent of the meals her mother had made when they'd had visitors during her childhood.

She, and the visitors and the children all ate dinner. The visitors remained silent through the meal, then thanked Ellen politely and left.

Ellen, still utterly confused by the whole experience, began to clean up the kitchen. As she picked up her mother's recipe book, and a piece of paper, yellowed with age fell out.

On it was written a verse:

Beware whene're you
deal with the Fae,
whether good or ill
they'll always repay.

Fae were fairies weren't they? Ellen tried to imagine that men who looked like serious bodybuilders might be fairies. That could explain the extra food magically appearing, she supposed.

So, dear Reader, we leave Ellen trying to understand her suddenly refilled pantry and freezer. She's going to be even more confused when she discovers her bank account's been refilled as well. It makes you wonder, what might have happened if she'd gone with her first impulse to refuse them hospitality.

The Stranger

Settle in, dear Reader, while I tell you the strange tale of two friends who had a strange encounter in the pub, that had nothing to do with how much they'd been drinking.

Keith and Evan, both in their mid-twenties, would get together at the local pub every Friday after work. It was a tradition they had started when they were eighteen.

Sometimes, one of them would bring another friend. So it was no surprise to either the evening a third person, who looked to also be in his mid twenties, joined them. Each of them mistakenly thought the other had invited them. He introduced himself as William.

Keith bought the first round of drinks. He started to talk about an issue he had with his sister. The other two sympathised with his plight of having to deal with her.

Evan brought the next round of drinks.

The stranger said he also had issues with his sister. When his sister was twenty-five, she had published a book. It was the worst book ever written. Hardly anyone bought it, and those who did left terrible reviews. Then when she was seventeen, she'd gone completely nuts over no-one reading her book, and had yelled at every family member she was in contact with because they'd never encouraged their friends to buy it. When she was twenty-eight, she'd built a massive pile of the books in her parents' lounge room and set fire to it.

Keith said, "Wait, if she published the book when she was twenty-five, how could she get mad about it when she was seventeen?"

William was quiet a moment then said, in a tone that suggested a sudden realisation, "This is the early twenty-first century, isn't it?"

Keith and Evan both looked confused.

William said, "I should go." He got up to leave.

Evan said, "Hey, it's your shout."

William stood strangely still, and stared straight ahead as if he was seeing something they couldn't. He said, "Shout: to yell. No, that's not appropriate. Shout, colloquial twentieth and twenty-first century: to purchase a round of drinks."

He pulled two small gold discs out of his pocket, and put them on the table, and said, "This should cover the cost of my shout." Then he turned and left.

Keith and Evan looked at the gold discs. They were coins of a type they had never seen.

"Do you think they're real gold?" Keith said, eventually.

"Maybe? I wonder how you find out. One of us should google that. You're friend is really weird."

"I thought he was your friend."

Well, dear Reader, they were actual gold coins. I'm sure you won't be surprised to find they were worth far more than a round of drinks.

Twenty years later, Evan and Keith were having their weekly drink at the pub, and were surprised to find William was there. He still looked as if he were in his mid-twenties.

Evan said, "You don't look like you've aged at all. I've got to tell you, when we met you here before, you almost had us believing you were some kind of time traveller."

William said, "I have currency from your time now, I'll shout first." The other two laughed, but he didn't.

While he was at the bar getting drinks, Evan and Keith talked about how weird he was.

Keith asked what William did for a living.

"I'm a history teacher. I like to do my own in-person research, so I do a bit of travelling in my time off."

Keith dared to ask when William was a history teacher.

William laughed, and said, "Not yet. I'm off now. Maybe I'll see you some time in the future."

So, dear Reader, we leave Keith and Evan, wondering if their acquaintance really is a time-travelling history teacher, or if they are the victims of a very long-running practical joke.

Headache

I invite you dear Reader to get comfortable. Settle in while I tell you the strange tale of Andrea who had a weird dream and an awful headache.

Andrea didn't know how she got here. Her head was aching and nothing seemed quite real. She decided it was a dream. She was among a group of about twenty people and they were building sandcastles. Why they were building sandcastles, she didn't know, but she knew she was determined to make the best sandcastle she could. Apart from damp sand, differently shaped buckets and a small toy spade, there were decorative things like seashells available.

Others were making fairly standard castles, with turrets, drawbridges and such. Andrea did something different. She sculpted a dragon of sand, using small roundish shells as eyes. She used a stick to draw individual scales and other features on the beast.

Things went fuzzy as her headache intensified. Then she found herself running some kind of obstacle course. She jumped over things, crawled under things, climbed up things, slid down things, not knowing why, only knowing her head ached.

Again, everything went fuzzy, and she found herself singing karaoke. Never a singer, she decided to just lean into it. It was a dream after all. So she gave it her all, singing her heart out despite her pounding headache.

Things went fuzzy again.

She found herself with the other people on a stage. A crowd of people were yelling and cheering for them. A woman was standing on the stage in front of them. Andrea couldn't make out what the woman was saying, her head was pounding so much.

The woman had turned to look at her. The people beside her were pushing her forward.

Andrea walked, hesitantly, to the front of the stage, as the crowd yelled even louder, making her headache so much worse.

The woman handed her microphone to Andrea. Apparently, she was meant to say something. Say what?

It was a dream. It didn't matter what she said. Andrea looked at the crowd, then at the microphone and said, "Well, all that was weird wasn't it?"

The crowd yelled and screamed.

"I don't know what do you guys think?"

She held the microphone toward the crowd and they yelled even louder.

Andrea gave the microphone back, saying, "What they said."

The crowd yelled and screamed even more. Andrea felt sick. The headache was so intense she thought she was going to pass out.

Some more people came on stage, carrying a huge novelty cheque. They held it up in front of Andrea, at waist-to-chest. height. She obligingly grabbed hold of it as well. Everything went fuzzy again.

We'll leave Andrea for a while to sleep peacefully now, dear Reader, as that headache has become very bad.

Andrea woke, checked her phone and realised it was Monday. Had she slept a whole weekend? Did she just not remember what she'd done on Saturday and Sunday? The headache was not quite as intense, but was still there.

She ate cereal and dressed for work.

Arriving in the office, she found people were staring at her.

"I thought you had another week off," someone said.

"I thought you might just quit and retire on your winnings," another said.

Her boss called her into his office. "You're back a week early, you still have another week's holiday," he said.

"Sorry," she said. "I must have got confused. I've got a horrible headache."

"Maybe go home and get some rest then. You must need a rest anyway. I really thought you were going to be out of the game when that horse threw you, then kicked your head as it ran away."

"I don't remember a horse," she said. The headache was intensifying, everything was going fuzzy again.

Andrea woke up in a hospital bed.

"You had a bleed on the brain," a nurse said. "Probably from that horse kick. You're going to be fine now."

Andrea's head still ached, but it was nowhere near as bad.

"I don't remember a horse," she said. Hadn't she said that sentence before? When was that? She had no clear memory of the recent past, just some snatches of strange things.

"I saw that kick on the tv and thought you had to have a concussion. I thought there was no way they'd let you keep playing. But the doctor cleared you, and the next night you were building sandcastles with the rest of them. Obviously their doctor didn't know what he was doing. I voted for you, though. I voted you from the beginning, but after the horse, I voted four or five times a day."

Voted? What was that about? Out loud, she managed to say, "Thanks."

"Did you actually see yourself? I'm pretty sure it's all on catch-up," the nurse said. "The in-room tv has catch up on the free to air channels."

The nurse left. Andrea picked up the tv remote and scrolled through its menu.

She found a recently-completed series called, "Two Weeks of Whatever." It was a reality program in which contestants were given a series of unrelated challenges, every day for a fortnight. The selling point was each day's activities were broadcast the same night.

Andrea watched the series, watching herself as one of a group of twenty people, taking part in a seemingly random series of activities. Each episode had a tally of votes on the bottom of the screen.

Votes for her had been average, around the same as everyone else, up until an episode four where they went horse-riding. Her horse had, indeed, thrown her and kicked her in the head while running away. Then, her votes had increased far over the other competitors, increasing by a larger and larger amount each night.

After watching the first week, Andrea was exhausted, and went back to sleep.

So, dear Reader, we leave Andrea, confused as to why a head injury would make her so insanely popular. Eventually, she's going to get to the end of the nonsense, and then check her bank account. She will discover she really did win a million dollars, and all it took was a near-fatal head injury.

Love Potion

Comfortable, dear Reader? Ready for another story? This time it's the story of Katrina, who just wanted the boy she liked to like her back.

Katrina was the kind of sixteen year old who spent more time in the library than on the sporting field. To put it bluntly, she was a nerd. She got great grades, played piano instead of sport, and was captain of the debating team.

It was a surprise for everyone who knew her when she fell, hard, for the captain of the cricket team. Gary was not known for good grades. He was known for great bowling.

Her mother thought it was "cute" that she had her "first crush". For Katrina it was far from cute. It was a crushing weight that seemed about to suffocate her. It was an epic love that would outlive the mountains. If only he would actually acknowledge her existence!

There was a school dance coming up. Katrina resolved to be brave. She approached Gary, and asked, hesitatingly, if he would like to go with her. Gary looked at her as if she was something he'd stepped in, and then laughed. Then he called over his friend Carl, and told him what Katrina had said. Carl joined in the laughter.

For the rest of the day, any time Katrina found herself in the same space as boys from the cricket team, she would hear whispers and laughter.

She was desperate to get away from school that afternoon. Her friend, Lucia, wanted to go to the shops on the way home. Katrina was hesitant, afraid they'd encounter more of Gary's friends.

Lucia said, "Forget about him. You can do better. You can definitely do smarter."

Katrina said, miserably, "But I don't want better or smarter."

"Look, Kat. His only skill is throwing a ball fast. He's good for high school, but he's not good enough to be a pro player. So what's he going to do with his life? Come on! I guarantee in ten years' time, if you bump into him, you're going to realise he peaked in high school. He's a jerk, so are his friends, and you are a genius. You are a queen and you are going to rule. So straighten that crown, ignore them, and let's get some retail therapy."

Katrina sighed, and said, "You're probably right, but I just really like him, and I wish I could make him like me as well."

In the centre area of the local shopping centre, there was a space for visiting pop up shops.

On this day, there was a strange stand, with endless tiny bottles. A sign, that was written in black glitter against a background of silver glitter, simply said: "Potions."

Of course, dear Reader, neither girl thought magic potions were real. They were smart young women, after all.

The woman sitting behind the table called out to Katrina, "Having a bad day, deerie? I'll give you a love potion for free."

Lucia giggled. Katrina answered the woman, "What's the catch?"

I told you she was smart, dear Reader. She already knew nothing was ever free.

The woman smiled and said, "The love potion is free, but the antidote is fifty dollars."

Katrina and Lucia both laughed.

Lucia asked, "Why would she need an antidote?"

The old woman smiled more broadly, as if she was sharing the joke. "Love is a powerful thing. You can't control it. Sometimes you want it to stop. Take the love potion deerie.

169

Just a little drop behind each of your ears is all it takes. I'm here til tomorrow, if you want the antidote."

She handed Katrina a tiny, heart-shaped pink bottle, with glitter all over it.

Katrina put it in her uniform pocket, and thanked the woman politely.

The next morning, Katrina looked at the tiny bottle. It was probably cheap perfume, from the look of the bottle. She was about to throw it out, but decided to find out what it smelled like, first.

She opened the bottle held it under her nose and inhaled. It was heavenly. It was the most wonderful thing she had ever smelled. She put a drop behind each ear as instructed.

Over breakfast, both of her parents seemed entranced. They both neglected their food, and just looked at her, lovingly, while she ate her cereal.

"OK," she said. "I've got to be off."

Her father broke his trance to say, "I could drive you to school today, if you like."

"Thanks, but you always say it's too far out of your way to drop me off before you go to work."

"I'm so sorry for that. I should never have disappointed you like that. I'll do better."

Katrina thought it was weird, but she accepted the ride. She had to keep telling her father to look at the road instead of at her.

When he parked the car, he got out and walked up to the school gate with her. Katrina started to wonder if her father might be having some sort of crisis. He stopped at the school gate and watched her go up the path towards her home room.

Just before she made it to the class room, Gary came rushing up to her. He apologised profusely for the previous day. He didn't know what had come over him. Would she please, please, please, go to the dance with him? He knew she might have already agreed to go with someone else, but if she hadn't, could she please go with him?

Katrina was confused. Was this some kind of trick, some prank to humiliate her further?

Before she could answer, Carl had pushed between Gary and Katrina. He gave Gary a hard shove to get him out of the way.

"Forget that loser," Carl said. "Come to the dance with me. I'll do anything if you'll just come with me."

Gary shoved Carl back. Before Katrina knew what was happening, the two were having an all out fight.

She rushed past them, and into the classroom. Her home room teacher Mr Curtis dropped the book he was holding. He walked over to her, appearing to be in the same kind of daze her father had been. "Katrina," he said. "You're looking lovely today. Radiant, in fact. I don't think I've ever really **seen** you before. I mean of course, I've seen you, but I haven't **seen** you. You see what I mean?"

"Ah, yes, sir, I see." She did not see, not at all.

"Oh, Katrina, you don't have to call me 'Sir', to you, I'm Geoffrey, or Geoff, or anything else you want to call me. Call me your slave."

Katrina backed away. "I've just remembered, I had to go to, to … to the office! I've still got time, haven't I? Before home room?"

"For you, my angel, there is all the time in the world."

Katrina fled the room.

She ran straight into Lucia.

"Ooof! Careful there," Lucia said.

"Everyone's gone insane! Carl and Gary are fighting, Mr Curtis told me to call him by his first name and said I was radiant. I have to get out of here!"

Two more of the cricket team members saw Katrina and rushed over to squabble over who was asking her to the dance. Gary heard them, and those two were drawn into the fight, which had gathered a crowd.

The crowd, however, now seeing Katrina directed attention at her. People were wanting to talk to her, wanting to touch her, telling her how much the admired or even adored her.

Lucia hissed, "Did you use that stupid potion?"

Katrina practically cried, "Yes."

"We've got to get the antidote."

"I know I need it, but where am I going to get fifty dollars?"

Mr Curtis was behind her. "You need money, my sweetness?" He pulled out his wallet and handed her three twenty dollar notes. "I don't usually carry much cash. I can go to the teller machine and get more if you want it."

Katrina grabbed the money. "No, thank you, Sir, I mean Geoffrey, this is all I need. So very kind of you. I promise I'll pay you back."

He waved a hand in a dismissive manner, "No need to repay me. What is money compared to your exquisite beauty?"

"Sir, Geoffrey, can Lucia and I please leave the school grounds? We won't be long."

"Of course, my precious one. You may do whatever your heart desires."

"Thanks, Sir," Lucia said, as she grabbed Katrina's arm and dragged her out of the building towards the shopping centre. The crowd followed.

At the old woman's stall, Katrina held out the cash and said, "I need the antidote! I need it now! Please!"

The old woman said, "That will be a hundred dollars, deerie."

Katrina said, "But it was fifty yesterday!"

The woman smiled showing the few remaining teeth in there mouth. "Supply and demand, deerie. Yesterday it wasn't in demand. Today it is."

Lucia practically spat: "You horrible old cow!"

The woman laughed.

Katrina said to the crowd, "I need more money. Can anyone loan me money? I'll pay it back next week."

A man walking past the chaos stopped, and offered her his credit card.

The old woman said, "That will do," and snatched the card. She processed the transaction, gave the man back his card, and gave Katrina another small bottle.

"Behind the ears, like the other," the woman said.

Katrina immediately complied.

Suddenly the crowd of followers all looked at each other in an utterly confused manner. The man looked down at his credit card, looked at Katrina and at the old woman, put his card back in his wallet, and walked away, fast.

Katrina and Lucia slowly walked back to the school.

Katrina said, "Why didn't you go crazy, the same as everyone else?"

Lucia replied, "I'm your best friend. I already love you more than everyone else does. We can go to the dance together, you know. We don't need dates."

"Thanks. I think I'm going to plan on not trying to date anyone for a while."

So, dear Reader, we leave Katrina, who has learned that trying to compel someone to love her was a mistake. There's going to be some awkward conversations around the school, as Katrina returns the money she borrowed from her teacher, and the cricket team members have to explain the brawl in the hall to a very angry principal.

Body Count

I invite you dear Reader to get comfortable. Settle in while I take you to the not too distant future to tell you the strange tale of Lexi, who just wanted what many people want, to find love.

Lexi had met Jason online. They'd talked for a while, and were going to meet for the first time, for coffee.

Entering the coffee shop, Lexi looked around. She saw Jason already there. He stood up to greet her as she approached.

When they were seated, his first words were, "So what's your body count?"

"I'm sorry, what?"She asked.

"You work for Sicarius."

"How did you know that?"

"I've done my research."

"So you're not interested in me, personally."

"How many people have you killed?"

"You've done your research badly. I'm R and R. Research and referrals. I'm just the person who researches the targets, makes sure they're not on the no-go list, and studies them, and learns about their habits, where they're likely to be when, that type of thing. Then I refer to an assassin."

"You're still involved in the murders."

"Not murders. Murder is a legal term, for an intentional, illegal killing. Since the Population Reduction Act was passed into law, assassination is legal, except in the special cases on the no-go list."

"Legally, you're not a murderer. Morally you are."

"I don't kill anyone."

"You're contributing to it. You're a part of it."

"So you invited me here, making it seem like a date, to dump on my job?"

"No. I want someone killed."

"Then call the office and make an intake appointment, like everyone else."

Lexi stood up, picked up her handbag, and prepared to leave.

"Stop, please," he said.

"Why?"

"It's not a regular assassination. I need someone who can kill, but who has some empathy. You seemed to be the right person when we were talking online. Please, let me tell you what's happening."

Lexi sat again. "You've got five minutes," she said.

"I have cancer. It's an aggressive type. Inoperable. I'm sick, and it's getting worse. The meds for pain make me nauseous. There's no hope of getting better. I want to die."

"You can go to a doctor for medically assisted suicide."

"I have a younger sister. I raised her since our parents died when she was ten. She's going to need my life insurance. It won't pay out if I kill myself, but it will if someone else kills me."

"It won't pay out if you hire someone else to kill you either."

"That's where the empathy comes in. Can you please just kill me, and leave one of those cards to say it was a paid assassination?"

"You're not on the no-go list?"

"I'm not important to anyone except my sister. I'm not on the list."

176

"My body count is zero. I've never actually killed anyone. Maybe you're right and I'm morally responsible, but I still haven't actually killed anyone. I don't think I could."

"Do you have an assassin you could assign the job to?"

"Payment would have to come from somewhere. Can you persuade your sister to order the assassination?"

"She's sixteen. Not old enough."

"Can you order it? I'd give you the money. If you need a reason, say you came on a date and I was a jerk, whatever."

"Like you accused me of being a murderer because of my job?"

"Like that."

"Let me think about it."

"And, there's one other thing. My sister. Like I said, she's sixteen. The insurance will cover her expenses until she grows up, but she'll need someone to look out for her."

"You want me to order your death, then offer to help out your sister?"

"I know it's a lot to ask."

"I want to meet your sister, and know she's OK with this."

"Sure. She should be home from school now."

So, dear Reader, Lexi found herself going to Jason's house, to meet his little sister Leah.

Leah knew of her brother's plan and wasn't happy about it, but she did understand that he could not cope with increasing pain and illness. She said she respected his choice.

Lexi thought a while and said, "Well, this really is the absolute worst date I've ever had. Give me the money, I'll have you killed in a week's time. That gives you time to change your mind if you decide to go with hospice care instead."

Jason handed over the money, and both he and Leah thanked her.

Over the next week, Lexi checked in with both Leah and Jason every day. At the end of the week, Jason was shot. In accordance with Lexi's instructions, it was quick and clean, an instant death.

Lexi continued to stay in contact with Leah, who had lost her entire family.

It began with Lexi taking care of Leah, but it became a mutual friendship. Leah moved into Lexi's house, and they were more like sisters than friends.

And so, dear Reader, after having her date killed, Lexi found a different kind of love from the one she had gone looking for. She found the love of a best friend and sister.

Oxygen

Settle in dear Reader, get comfortable, while I tell you the strange tale of Alice who was a bit over-worked, and admittedly needed a rest.

Alice worked full time in a corporate gristmill. Her sister Merrill had opted out of the grind and sold herbs and crystals.

After a particularly tough week, Alice had a visit from her sister. "I know you're struggling and need to relax, so I've booked us in for an oxygen therapy session," Merrill said.

"Oxygen therapy? What's that?" Alice asked.

"We take in oxygen, and breathe out all the things we don't need."

"So, like, breathing? Yeah, I do that most of the time anyway. We have to be booked in somewhere for it?"

"There's more to it than that. Come on. This is going to be transformative."

"Transformative? What will we transform into?"

"Don't be silly, come on."

Merrill took her sister to a small shop in a shopping centre. The air was heavy with some kind of incense.

"We're meant to breathe in this?"

"It's to help you relax," Merrill answered. "Just be nice and don't criticise everything. That cynicism's why you're so stressed."

"Really? I thought it was because I was trying to do a hundred hours work in a forty hour week."

"This must be Shantara, our therapist."

A woman half buried in beads greeted them and had them sit in large armchairs. She pushed buttons on the chairs, which reclined, and a massage program began.

"Massage chairs. I could handle this," Alice said, "but I wish those cats outside would stop yowling and fighting."

"That's music. Be nice," Merrill hissed.

Shantara gave them each a plastic oxygen mask to put on their faces.

"At least the plastic smell overwhelms the incense," Alice said.

"Just relax," Merrill said. "Go with it. You've got to give it a chance. It's an experience."

Shantara said, "Now ladies, just inhale deeply of the pure clean oxygen, exhale all of the bad feelings, the things that tire you out."

"I usually exhale carbon dioxide," Alice said.

Merrill hissed at her to be quiet.

Shantara said, "Smell that sweet, sweet oxygen."

"Still just smelling plastic," Alice said.

"Just breathe and relax," Shantara said. She dimmed the lights and turned up the cat yowl music.

"Wow, just what I needed on my day off, the experience of being treated for pneumonia."

"Be quiet. I don't know why I bring you for things like this," Merrill said.

"I don't know either," Alice answered.

"I'm not answering any more," Merrill said. "Just relax."

Alice tried to relax. The massage chair was quite nice, but the music was grating on her nerves, and the smell of plastic was making her feel sick, and she could feel her mouth and nose drying from the oxygen being pumped into her face.

180

She tried to relax, to lean into the massage and ignore the rest of the nonsense.

As she watched the ceiling, she saw things float across her vision. She'd had floaters in her eyes before, tiny specs of nothing floating past her eyes, and often thought of getting her eyes checked, but never had the time.

As she watched, they seemed more planned than the random spots she'd seen in the past. These, although they looked similar, did not seem so random. Looking like amoebas, the floated around, sometimes joining with each other, sometimes splitting. They seemed to be performing a choreographed dance routine.

Alice lost track of time. She stopped noticing the smell of plastic. The yowling and screeching music seemed to actually suit the strange hypnotic dance she was observing.

And so, dear Reader, Alice lost track of time, and while it was only an hour before Shantara returned, it could have been days for all Alice knew.

Alice felt like she was coming back from a long way away, from the deepest of sleeps, as the massage stopped and the chair returned her to the upright seated position.

She saw Merrill beside her and smiled.

"Take off your masks now. Make sure you're feeling that you've fully returned before you get up, to leave," Shantara said. She left them again

"I'm just so relaxed. I feel so rested," Alice said. "I'm amazed."

"Oh stop," Merrill said. "OK you were right. This was stupid. An hour of listening to yowling and sniffing plastic was a nightmare."

"No, I'm serious. I feel like I've caught up on weeks of sleep."

"Stop making fun of me. Let's go and get lunch."

So dear Reader, we leave the sisters, who have each had a change of perspective about fad therapies.

Living a Fairy Tale

"Once upon a time…" So many beloved childhood stories, dear Reader, began with those magical words. Beginning with those words we read wondrous stories. A girl broke into the three bears' home, ate their food, broke their furniture, and escaped without penalty. A big bad wolf eats Grandma, and in turn gets killed. A man kisses a sleeping princess without her consent, but since he's rich and apparently handsome, it's OK. In a similar story a rich, handsome young man, kisses a dead girl, and that's OK too. Those were just the versions of the stories sanitised for children's consumption. The originals were often far, far, worse.

Somehow, however, people remember fairy tales with great affection, none more so than Astrid, who dreamed of some magical intervention, and the arrival of her handsome prince.

Astrid worked on the perfume counter of a well-known department store. It had seemed a romantic job when she'd taken it. She'd gained that idea from a movie. In fact it wasn't romantic. Her feet and legs ached from standing all day. She'd gained a permanent pain in her lower back. The perfumes gave her hay fever. The customers were the nastiest, most entitled people she'd ever met.

Despite the distinct lack of romance in the "romantic" job she'd chosen for herself, Astrid still dreamed of her handsome prince, and her happily ever after. Surely some day her Prince Charming would come for her.

One night, after a particularly tiresome day at work, she wished on a star. It wasn't a particular star, not a falling or shooting star, or even the first star of the night because she hadn't been watching the sky. But the thought occurred to her to wish on a star, and she did.

Astrid went to bed dreaming of her handsome prince coming to save her from her the horrible job she'd chosen for herself.

The next day, a handsome man in a suit came to the perfume counter. He was looking for a gift for his mother. He and Astrid compared perfumes. Astrid suspected he was flirting, and knew he was when he asked for her number. Was this her Prince Charming?

Let's fast forward this, dear Reader, they dated, it was a whirlwind romance, and eventually they were engaged. Astrid was so fixated on her happily ever after, she missed a pile of red flags along the way.

One evening, Astrid was cooking dinner, while Prince Charming sat in front of the television. "Can you please set the table?" Astrid asked.

"No," he answered. "I'm busy."

"Doing what?"

"Doesn't matter. I'm busy. Stop being lazy and passing your work on to me."

"Why is it my work?"

"Because you're the woman. You do the work in the house. I need to rest because I've been at work all day."

"I've been at work all day, too. You sit at a desk, and I stand up all day. So I need a rest more than you do."

"Nah, that's not how it works."

This were finally clicked for Astrid. She could see the things she'd ignored up until this point.

"And in the rules of how it works, is there a rule that says you should contribute financially to the household at all? Want to help with electricity, rent, groceries, anything?"

"Stop nagging."

"Nagging? This is the first time I've said anything, and I really should have before now. This is not how I'm going to live the rest of my life. So unless you're going to pull your weight in this relationship, you can get out of my flat."

"You can't just kick me out."

"Watch me."

That, dear Reader, was when Astrid learned that the only way she was going to be rescued was if she rescued herself. She took some courses, studied management, and got a better job. She established a life she enjoyed, and learned to rely on herself. Some time later, she would meet, not a prince, but a decent man, who she would marry, and they would live, mostly happily, ever after. It wasn't a romantic fairy tale, but it was a good life.

Pencils

I invite you, dear Reader, to settle in, get comfortable, while I tell you the strange tale of Delia, who simply wanted art supplies, but got far more than she expected.

Delia was perusing the shelves at the Art Supply Shack, where she noticed a brand of pencils she hadn't seen before. They were labelled "Cartoonists' Colour."

She asked Gail, who owned the shop, "These new ones, are they any good?"

Gail looked at the pencils. She said, "They're specialty cartoonists' pencils. They're not designed for your usual work."

"What's the difference?"

"Well, you need to know the rules of cartoons to use the cartoon ones."

"The rules of cartoons?"

"Well, yes. Cartoon drawing has movement. It doesn't just stand still on the page."

"I did a unit on animation at art school. The movement comes from images being shown in quick succession. Persistence of vision makes them appear to move, rather than be individual images. Pencils aren't going to make anything move."

Delia bought the pencils, because she loved trying new brands and styles of art supplies.

At home, she took the pencils, and a sheet of drawing paper, and drew a quick sketch of her cat, Miss Fluffybuns, patting a ball of wool. The pencils were soft and made strong marks. Delia was impressed, and enjoyed working with them.

She put the drawing down and went to make herself a cup of coffee.

Something happened while she was out of the room, dear Reader, something that Delia would never be able to rationalise, nor forget.

She came back to her art studio with her coffee, to find the drawing moving on the page. The drawn Miss Fluffybuns was patting the ball across the page and back.

Delia watched her drawing play, while she drank her coffee, not sure what to make of it.

The real Miss Fluffybuns came to investigate. She did not know what to make of it either, but was disturbed by it. Her whole life had been spent watching Delia create art, and this had never happened before. She began yowling and patting at the paper.

That was when the drawing pulled itself up off the paper, and pounced on Miss Fluffybuns, biting and scratching at her. The real Miss Fluffybuns jumped and ran, the drawn one chasing her.

Delia gave chase. She gulped down the last of her coffee, and tried to use the empty cup, inverted, to catch the cartoon cat. That cat simply flattened itself, and as a mobile drawing on the floor tiles slid out from under the mug, and went back to chasing the traumatised, real cat. By now the cartoon had pulled a giant cleaver out of a pocket Delia had not drawn.

"The rules of cartoons," that was what Gail had said. Of course in cartoons, animated creatures could just pull weapons, or tools, or anything else, out of anywhere. What were the other rules of cartoons? How could they help here?

Delia began to think of Acme branded explosives, that always worked against the person using them, not the intended target. She thought of pianos and anvils dropped from great heights. She thought of doors drawn in walls that could be opened… which led her to think of a solution.

She grabbed a black pencil. With a circle and some shading, she drew a big hole in the tiled floor. Then she called Miss Fluffybuns to her. As Miss Fluffybuns was about to run across the drawn hole in the floor, Delia scooped her up in her arms.

The cartoon Fluffybuns ran halfway across the drawing of a hole in the floor, then looked down. After looking down it had a shocked expression for a moment, then dropped into the hole.

"The rules of cartoons," Delia said to the trembling cat in her arms, "say that cartoons can walk or run on air, until they look down."

She kept holding Miss Fluffybuns tightly to her chest with one hand, as she went to her work table and picked up an eraser with the other hand. Still soothing the cat, she began to erase the hole on the floor, starting from the centre, working carefully outward, being sure to erase all sign of the cartoon cat before finally erasing the hole it had fallen down.

I'm sure you won't be surprised, dear Reader, to learn that those Cartoonists' Colour pencils were used as kindling in the back yard barbecue, and Delia has never been remotely interested in buying anything more in the range. Miss Fluffybuns was not physically hurt, and has mostly recovered from her shock, but now avoids the art studio.

Hand

Settle in dear Reader, while I tell you the strange tale of Evelyn, who learned that dreams can become nightmares.

Evelyn had a dream.

As dreams go it was a simple one: she would have a little house just outside of the city. It would be brick, for better insulation, and have solar power. It would be as far off grid as it was possible to get in the modern world.

She would grow her own vegetables and fruit, raise chickens, and live a simple life. The resources of the city would be close by if she needed them, but mostly she would keep to herself and enjoy the quiet of her home.

That was the whole of her dream. She didn't want to use the quiet to write a book, or start a cult, or prepare for the apocalypse, or do anything grandiose, or paranoid, or outstanding or unusual in any way. She just wanted the quiet of the country, with the resources of a city nearby.

Evelyn worked hard, lived minimally, and saved as much as she could to meet her dream.

Sadly, many others had similar dreams, and the cost of little homes just outside of the city increased faster than her savings.

One day, when her lounge chairs had outlived their usefulness to the point of being painfully uncomfortable, she went to a second-hand shop. Evelyn, thinking of her savings and her dream, never bought new if second-hand was available.

She found a suite, a three seater and two armchairs, which looked much nicer than her old one. Sitting in each one, she found them comfortable. Evelyn cringed a little at the price, but realised that it would be at least three times the price new. There was definitely enough money in her savings. She had plenty of money, just not "buying a house on the outskirts of the city" money.

Approaching the counter to pay and arrange delivery, something caught her eye.

It was ugly. It was offensive. It was hideous. It was hypnotic. It seemed to call to her. It demanded her attention. It looked like a tiny hairy hand, shrivelled and desiccated.

"Ah, you've seen my most unique treasure," the salesman said, seeing her staring at the object. "You don't get these around much any more. It's only legal because it was made before the law was changed. It's a mummified monkey hand. A great talking point at parties, and there's a legend it will grant wishes, four wishes, one for each finger. The thumb doesn't count. But of course it's just a legend."

Evelyn did not need a mummified monkey's hand. Never in her life had she ever thought: "I want a mummified monkey's hand." Looking at the hideous object, she felt nauseous, repelled, and yet... There was just something. If she'd been asked, she wouldn't have been able to say why she did it.

She bought the monkey's hand, as well as the lounge suite.

Somehow, she failed to notice the salesman putting on gloves and using a pair of tongs to pick up the paw and put it in a paper bag, before wrapping the bag in tissue paper and placing that in another bag to hand over to her.

At home, Evelyn carefully unwrapped the hand, and put in on her fairly bare bookshelf. Evelyn loved to read, but why buy books when the library was free?

She stared, transfixed, at the ugly, hairy hand. "You grant wishes do you?" she asked. "I wish you could give me the money to buy my dream house." Nothing happened. There was no flash of light, no roll of thunder, nothing whatsoever.

Of course nothing happened. No inanimate object had the power to grant wishes, or anything else. It was just a stupid myth.

Beware, dear Reader, of anyone, or anything, which offers to give you something with nothing in return. There is always a cost.

While Evelyn was eating dinner that night, she received a phone call. Her beloved mother had died. With tears in her eyes, she looked over at the bookshelf, to see the monkey's index finger had curled, leaving the other three fingers upright.

In the next few days, and weeks, Evelyn was overwhelmed with organising a funeral, discovering she had inherited all of her mother's money and possessions, and the emotional rollercoaster of grief.

It was only months later, when her mother's house and other major possessions had been sold, sentimental pieces kept to be treasured, and other miscellaneous items given to charity, that Evelyn realised she now had enough money to buy her dream home.

After moving, Evelyn found herself wondering if the monkey's hand had somehow caused her mother's death. It was a stupid idea, and yet, the death had happened so soon after she'd made that wish, and the death had eventually led to her buying her house.

She searched online for the myth the salesman had mentioned, and found the W.W. Jacobs short story *The Monkey's Paw*. With horror, she read, the characters in the story had also first wished for money, and gained it via a death of a loved one.

Evelyn picked up the hand, with its one curled and three outstretched fingers, took it outside and threw it in the council wheelie bin. She felt as if an imposing weight lifted from the atmosphere around her, as if she'd been carrying something heavy all day, and hadn't realised the weight until she put it down.

That night she slept better than she'd done since her mother died. In the morning she continued to lie lazily in bed while she listened to the rubbish truck empty her bin. The horrible, fascinating, object was gone, and life would be good from here on in.

She was so happy she almost skipped to the kitchen for breakfast, but there, on the kitchen bench, was the hand.

Evelyn put the hand in an old shoe box, dug a hole in the yard, and buried it.

The next day, the grass for about a metre around the buried box was dead. A day later it was two metres. The day after that, it was three metres, encroaching on the chicken coup, and the chooks were sick.

Evelyn dug the box up again, took out the hand, and took it back inside.

The dead areas of grass did not heal, and nothing she planted would grow there. The chooks all died.

Evelyn bought more hens, and built a new pen for them further from the house. She also bought a dog for companionship.

She tried to not see the hideous hand as she walked past it numerous times each day, and concentrated on living the life she'd dreamed of. She planted her vegetables, and her fruit trees. She nurtured them, checking on each plant and tree each day, her faithful dog walking by her side. She fed the chooks, and gathered eggs, and the dog learned to carry the egg basket for her.

One morning she woke, to the sound of her dog whining. It was lying on the floor, paws over its face, muzzle covered in black slime. Beside it was the hand. No. She could not save her faithful friend share the fate of the first chooks. She picked up the hand and made her wish. "I wish I'd never seen this horrible thing."

Evelyn was back in the second hand shop, looking at a lounge suite that might meet her needs. She was dismayed by the price, but realised it was good value.

Returning to her small rented flat, she phoned her mother and chatted about everything of passing interest and nothing of note.

Life continued as it always had, but Evelyn found she no longer wanted her little house outside of the city. With her savings, she was able to put a deposit on quite a reasonable house in a less expensive suburb, and be able to buy herself some of the little luxuries she'd always denied herself. She also developed a habit of calling her mother every day.

So, dear Reader, we leave Evelyn, whose life has not turned out as planned, but is still not bad, apart from those strange dreams about a horrible little hand and a house where things just died.

Labyrinth

Settle in dear Reader, get comfortable, while I tell you the strange tale of Grace, who just went to buy a lamp, but found herself somewhere completely unexpected.

Grace needed a reading lamp, The light in her guest room that she was using as a work from home office wasn't great, and she'd been getting headaches.

She went to a shop well-known for meatballs, and furniture that had sleek lines and allen keys.

Grace followed the arrows on the floor taking her through the store. It was like a maze, she thought, or a labyrinth. A labyrinth had only one way to go, but a maze had options that then led to other options, and some blank walls. A labyrinth just went one way. Where had she heard that? She couldn't remember. Was it correct? How did she know if she didn't know what her source was? Grace was never sure if she really knew what she thought she knew. She was never confident in her own knowledge of many things.

Everything in the store had Swedish names.They could have translated them into English, Grace thought. Surely she couldn't be the only person who looked at these strange words, and couldn't imagine how to pronounce them properly. Of course it was part of the culture, not so much the Swedish culture, as the culture of the store. It went with the meatballs, the arrows on the floor directing the one way through the labyrinth, and even the Swedish food store at the end. The problem wasn't the store, or the language, it was a problem with her. She only knew one language. Of course, she'd picked up a smattering of words from other languages, but not enough for a conversation, or to read a story. She really was lacking.

Eventually, she reached the light fittings and lamps. She wandered through the section, looking for one that would fit her needs. In among them, she saw a small statuette. It was gold, half-human, and half-bull. A minotaur. That didn't belong there. If it belonged anywhere, it would be with the wide range of homewares and decor items, not among the lighting.

She picked it up. Greek mythology. It was discordant. It didn't belong. It didn't fit the culture of the place. Of course, she could have been wrong about the culture of the store, and it really was just stuff shoved together by people too lazy to translate names of products to the local language.

Grace looked into the eyes of the small statue she held in her hand. Suddenly, she felt ill, nausea hit hard, and she found herself sweating, her whole body weak.

Feeling unwell, dear Reader, is surely to be expected when one suffers a temporal displacement.

Grace found herself facing a much larger, much more alive, Minotaur. She did what one would normally do in such a situation. She ran away. She was running down a tunnel, which had corners and turns, but no choices of direction. There was no light, but somehow she could see.

As she ran, gasping for breath, she knew she could not keep up this pace for long. She wondered if she wanted to keep going. This was the direction away from the beast, but the direction to where?

Was this the famed labyrinth of ancient Greece? If so, what did she know about it? She'd read somewhere it was actually a mine that went on and on, but she couldn't recall the source on that, and it could have been wrong. The labyrinth was a prison, wasn't it? It was a place to keep the minotaur, to prevent his escape. It stood to reason the path through the labyrinth wouldn't lead out, because the monster could just follow it and leave. If going the right direction in the labyrinth wouldn't take her outside, she'd have to go the wrong direction, back towards the monster. Was her reasoning right? What would the minotaur do if she approached it? It hadn't actually done anything, had it? She wasn't even sure it had given chase when she'd run. She'd just run and not looked back.

Grace caught her breath, then sighed deeply. She stood up straight and turned around. She began walking resolutely back the way she'd come.

Eventually, inevitably, she came to the minotaur, which was lumbering in the same direction it had been when she first saw it. It didn't make any move toward her, apart from staying on its course.

"Ah, hi," she said. Stupid, she thought to herself, of course it didn't speak English. How else should she communicate with it. "I need to go past you, that way," she pointed as she said it.

The monster stood still, looking at her, apparently confused.

"You might want to try that way too," she said, as she continued to point.

She approached, hesitantly. The monster didn't try to grab her or anything like that.

She pressed herself against the wall, and squeezed past the bull-headed creature. "This way, I mean, I think this is the way out," she said.

She reached for the creature's hand, and pulled it around to face the opposite direction to the way it had been facing. "Yes," she said, "this is the way. I'm almost sure of it." For once in her life, she did feel sure of something.

The minotaur started walking in the direction she was leading. They walked, and walked, following the tunnel as it turned and twisted. They walked, seemingly through time, as if nothing existed but the continual motion of one foot in front of the other. How had they gone so long without rest, without food? It had been days, weeks, possibly months or years. All Grace knew was grey walls, a darkness that was somehow light enough to see. She kept walking, the beast lumbering just behind her.

Then she saw it: light. It was not the strange light of the tunnel, but actual daylight. She had been right. When it really mattered, she had trusted her judgement, and she had been right.

She continued walking, and found the mouth of the tunnel, outside was a path, trees, flowering plants, and glorious sunlight.

She stepped through the entrance and was back in the lighting section of the shop.

Grace chose a lamp, and followed the arrows to the checkout.

So, dear Reader, we leave Grace, who had learned to trust her own judgment and knowledge.

That's all of our stories for now, dear Reader. I have to leave you now, but don't despair. I'll be back soon with more Strange Tales.